T0154228

SWEET
AFFLICTION

SWEET AFFLICTION

Anna Leventhal

Invisible Publishing

Halifax & Toronto

Text copyright © Anna Leventhal, 2014

All rights reserved. No part of this publication may
be reproduced or transmitted in any form, by any method,
without the prior written consent of the publisher.

Library and Archives Canada Cataloguing in Publication

Leventhal, Anna, 1979-, author
    Sweet affliction / Anna Leventhal.

Short stories.
ISBN 978-1-926743-43-1 (pbk.)

    I. Title.

PS8623.E9438S94 2014   C813'.6   C2014-900676-4

Cover & Interior designed by Megan Fildes

Typeset in Laurentian and Slate by Megan Fildes
With thanks to type designer Rod McDonald

Printed and bound in Canada

Invisible Publishing
Halifax & Toronto
www.invisiblepublishing.com

We acknowledge the support of the Canada Council for the Arts, which last year
invested $157 million to bring the arts to Canadians throughout the country.

Invisible Publishing recognizes the support of the Province of Nova Scotia
through the Department of Communities, Culture & Heritage. We are pleased
to work in partnership with the Culture Division to develop and promote our
cultural resources for all Nova Scotians.

For my parents

~

And in memory of Thompson Owens

There is no rest, really, there is no rest. There is just a joyous torment, all your life, of doing the wrong thing.

— Derek Walcott

~

Why do I always do the wrong thing in the middle of the night? I only want some attention.

— "Bomb Song", C. Hutchison

Gravity

The pregnancy test is called "Assure," except it's spelled "Asure," which kind of results in it having the opposite effect. I bring it to the cash and the checkout woman gives me this little wink and goes "Good luck," even though they're not supposed to make moralizing comments about your items.

The funny thing about buying a home pregnancy test is that you are holding your breath either way. It's just not a neutral purchase. So "good luck" is a safe bet because no matter what's intended, it applies. They should make two different kinds of pregnancy tests, one for women who really want to have a baby and one for everyone else. Each test would have the same two graphics: a bunch of exploding fireworks with the words *Way To Go* under it and, like, a frowny face. The same symbols for both tests, but for opposite results.

I walk across the parking lot to the car, where my parents and sister are waiting.

"All set?" says my dad.

I give him the thumbs up and strap myself in. I look over at Angela. She stares out the window, absent and solemn as a cat. We pull onto the highway and Mom turns the car toward my cousin's wedding.

My sister is in love with a man named Henry. I have always loved the name Henry, which is almost the same as being in love with a man named Henry, because when she says "I love Henry" I can think *Me too*.

All the boys my age have faces like half-baked buns. Henry's face has character. His face looks like it might have spent some time in the desert, surviving on cactus juice and lizards. Angela tells me he once got into a fist fight over the principle of a thing.

"What thing?" I say.

"Does it matter?"

"I guess not. Unless it's like Nazis or something."

"I think I ovulate just looking at him," Angela says.

Mom sometimes wonders out loud what Henry could want with a nineteen-year-old girl. But really, what couldn't he want? It seemed so obvious to me. Angela was it—the real deal, the whole enchilada. I came with her, like an accessory. It wasn't the worst position to be in. Where was Barbie without her pink high-heeled shoes, her pink vinyl purse? Broke and teetering.

We're not twins but I always thought we looked the same, that looking at Angela was like looking into a distorting mirror, a mirror of my future. We have the same wide-set eyes and square chins, and when we hit twelve, two years apart, we both got the same dusting of acne on our cheeks; I thought it made Angela even more beautiful because she looked tough and kind of oily, like a mink. But almost no one guesses that we're sisters.

Although she is beautiful beyond reason, Angela dresses like an Amish child because she can never find clothes she likes. My best friend Camille and I once followed her through the Le Château warehouse as she rejected every outfit we suggested with enough scorn to make us feel like we actually were raised in a trailer park on Mars. Angela is a genius of rejection, a grand master. She brings rejection to a new level. Her contempt covers areas unknown to regular women like our mother and her friends; knobby knees or "Hadassah arms" are problems miles beneath her criteria, which are obscure, baroque. Her disdain goes beyond regular language; she has to make up words to express it. She'll say things like "It's too froofy, I hate how it bargles like that at the collar, it makes my stomach all gronchy." I handed her a shirt the exact underside-of-a-cloud grey-blue of her eyes, and she snorted wearily. "I would look like David Cop-a-feel in that," she said. "I would look like Tom Ass Pinchin."

As soon as we cross into America the roads become smooth and gently curving, no longer the pockmarked highways of southern Quebec. The signs are different too. "This road maintained by Boy Scouts of America, Northampton Chapter," I read aloud. "This road maintained by Hoover Electric."

"Americans like to give their roads up for adoption," Dad says. "It's called neo-liberalism. You hand over responsibility for public infrastructure to private entities. Then if someone skids on a rough patch and breaks their neck, or throws out their transmission, you have someone to sue."

"The Boy Scouts of America?" I ask.

"More or less," he says. "It's about individual accountability. It's much easier to assign blame to a person or group of people than to a system or a class."

"This road maintained by Cheryl and Maude," I say.

Dad keeps talking about the erosion of the state's economic and social responsibility, and I stare out the window and think about Cheryl and Maude, and what kind of life

3

they have together. Do they live in a ramshackle bunga-low covered in wisteria vines? Is it decorated with Georgia O'Keeffe prints? They must have a pair of cats named Ger-trude and Alice. Why did they decide to become account-able for this stretch of Vermont highway? Was it, for them, like having a child?

I repeat the words "ramshackle bungalow" to myself, sa-vouring them. Angela cracks the window and lights a smoke.

As kids me and Angela used to squeeze each other's biceps, pretending they were breasts. "Nice rack," we'd say. We had a game we called "dating." We'd strip down to our panties and undershirts. Angela's was V-necked and had a small pink bow in the nadir of the V. Mine was plain and ribbed, like a boy's. Angela would put two clementines in her shirt, and I'd drop one down my undies. Then I'd take her on a date. This consisted of sitting side by side on my parents' brown corduroy sofa, me left and her right. Using a plate as a steer-ing wheel, I'd drive her around, maintaining a macho silence, while she'd talk about getting her hair done and the shoes she wanted to buy. Then she'd give me a directorial aside: "Try to make a move on me." And I'd go "Hey baby, enough chit-chat," and drop a hand onto her leg. She would slap it away and giggle, and I'd go back to driving, doing complicated three-point turns and flipping through channels on the radio.

"Try again," she'd whisper.

Once I reached a palm onto her leftmost clementine. It was awkward; I almost lost control of the car. Angela stared straight ahead with a look of grim concentration. Then she said, We're going off the road. I dropped the plate. It didn't break, it just rolled around on its rim for a while making a hollow croaking sound. If it had broken we would be different people, people who things happened to; I think we were both hoping it would break. But it didn't break.

Afterwards the backs of our thighs were pink and striped from the corduroy.

I never got past first base on those dates. But I liked the way the orange felt.

My cousin Jill, the one getting married, is thin and nervous, with fine hair and bug-eyes, like she's missing some kind of protective layer. She has horse teeth and a matching laugh and is altogether adorable. Once she told me she thought she might be gay because she had a poster of Linda Evangelista she couldn't stop staring at. "She's just so *radiant*," she had said. Now she's getting married to Harris, a skinny balding orthodontist who plays a lot of squash. He's the exact opposite of Linda Evangelista, but they seem totally bonkers for each other.

We pass an LED sign that says *Don't Drink and Drive!* For extra emphasis the *Don't* is blinking on and off, which means that half the time the sign says *Drink and Drive!* "God," Angela says, "I'm so dehydrated." Angela is never thirsty, only dehydrated. Dad pulls over to buy some bottled water and Mom disembarks for the gas station bathroom.

Still not looking at me, Angela says, "Did you get the goods?"

My best friend Camille once bought a home pregnancy test after she slept with a guy in the back of his truck outside the Orange Julep.

She took it in the bathroom of the mall because she was worried her family would see the box in the recycling bin and confront her about it. "They wouldn't have been mad," she said, "but my mom would have made this big feminist ceremony out of it, with like herbs and incense and ankh symbols, and I would have got a whole lecture on choice as the greater part of freedom and brave pioneering women and stuff like that. I wanted to keep it just for me."

Camille told me when she crouched over the little dip-stick and peed on it she was filled with a great sense of pride in her body. "It was this almost horny feeling," she said, "like I was some kind of ancient fertility goddess, fuck-ing and giving birth to all creation." Camille weighs about seventy pounds, is completely flat-chested, and looks like a pink-cheeked, tousle-haired boy, so it's hard to imagine her as any kind of sex goddess.

When the little plus sign appeared in the dipstick window, Camille went straight to a pay phone outside the food court and called the Morgentaler clinic. She told me that now whenever she hears the words "a woman's choice" she au-tomatically smells french fries.

"Got 'em," I tell Angela.

"You're a pal."

"You'd do the same for me."

She turns and looks at me, finally. "No, I would not. I would never let this happen to you. I would kill the guy first."

I say nothing.

"Anyway," she says. "It's not like *you* have to worry."

I pass her the plastic bag with the box in it and she stuffs it in her purse. Mom comes out of the bathroom and waves like she hasn't seen us in years.

We met Henry last fall, at a costume party someone had wit-tily titled The Communist Party. Everyone was wearing a fur hat or an eyeliner goatee, and I saw at least three ice picks in different head-stabbing configurations. I spent an hour trying to convince a dubious undergrad that I was dressed as false consciousness, and then I went looking for Angela.

She was talking to the only other person not in costume. He was wearing a plain black T-shirt and blue trousers in a way that let you know he had a nice body, but that he didn't put a lot of effort into it, at least not in the way other people do. He didn't go to the gym or play team sports, he had just gotten that way accidently, from building houses for political refugees or sandbagging flooding rivers. He was probably a volunteer firefighter or something.

"Ang," I said, "I want to go home."

"Stacey! I'm so glad you're here." As if she had just run into me by accident and we weren't like seventy-five percent of the same DNA.

"I want you to meet someone," she said, putting a hand on my arm. "Henry, Stacey, Stacey, Henry."

"I've always loved that name," I say.

"You guys must be sisters," he said. "You could be twins."

Not knowing how to respond, I sipped my beer. Angela giggled, but she looked a little pissed off, as though being recognized in this way threatened her personhood.

"I admit to a certain family resemblance," she said, tossing her hair a bit.

I don't remember what we talked about after that. Or what they talked about. I didn't talk. I felt like I was watching one of those old film reels of the atom bomb tests in Nevada, or a volcano erupting. That same feeling of helplessness and awe.

He asked if she wanted to hang out later and she said *k*. Just *k*. I thought, abcdefghijlmnopqrstuvwxyz. There are the rest of them. Maybe you could use them to make some more words. In fact, there are some useful words in there already, like *hi,* and also *no.* I didn't say this out loud.

Walking home neither of us said a thing. I thought about doing something extreme, making some grand gesture, like smashing a window or throwing myself under a bus. I felt ready for some really big emotion. Finally I worked up the courage to kick a pile of leaves. They were damp and instead of flying around everywhere they stuck to my sneaker and smelled perceptibly of dog shit. Angela didn't notice.

Angela once broke up with a guy because of something he said. He said, "The button fly. Girls always have trouble with the button fly." People thought she was frivolous, but really she just had a very strict aesthetic that was its own kind of moral order. Henry was different. He was like insulin. He created a need for himself that was almost chemical. I wanted to free her from him. But she didn't want to be freed.

A few hours in to the drive we stop at a scenic lookout—some ragged cliffs and a waterfall. My legs feel stiff and creaky. We hike to where the water crashes over the edge, so busy it makes you tired to look. Angela leans on the railing, facing us instead of the waterfall, like she's posing for a travel brochure.

There's a little girl being led down the path by the elbow, both hands covering her eyes. Halfway to the lookout she freezes, locking her knees and refusing to move. Her mother lets go of her arm and starts walking ahead.

"I'm going now!" she says. "Bye!"

The girl stays put, whimpering. Several hikers stop to try to talk to her, but every time they approach she takes a step backward, palms still pressed to her face.

A smiling middle-aged woman crouches beside the girl. "Don't be afraid of the waterfall, sweetie. It's very pretty."

"I hate pretty!" the girl shrieks.

By the time we get to the resort, a light drizzle is falling. My aunt Lydia is nearly in tears. The ceremony was supposed to be outside, by the lake, but a couple of guys in tuxes are herding everyone into banks of folding chairs inside the reception tent. Mom braces Lydia's shoulders and talks her down in a low cooing voice, like she's comforting a high-strung poodle. I sneak around the back of the boathouse and find Jill puffing a skinny menthol cigarette under the overhang, the hem of her dress rucked on the long grass.

"What happened to your face?" I say.

"It's airbrushed," she says. "All the girls do it now." Her hair is highlighted and set into sprayed sausage rolls on top of her head.

"You look gorgeous," I say.

"I feel like I'm gonna puke." We hug, her cool damp arms around me. Her cigarette is hovering dangerously close to her fire-hazard hair, so I pluck it out of her fingers and take a drag. She adjusts the top of her strapless dress, peering down at her cleavage. "I feel like a lemon meringue in this," she says.

"Where's Harris?"

She shrugs. "Some kind of groom thing. Out in the woods, playing bongos and beating his chest."

The idea of Harris performing any kind of masculinity ritual almost makes me laugh out loud, but then I can't help picturing him and Jill in the dark together, his skinny hairy fingers stroking her throat, his mouth inching crab-like along her thigh.

"You better go before you dissolve in the rain," I say.

She reaches out and pats my head. "Good old Stacey." I hand her back the smoke; she takes a last long drag and flicks the butt into the weeds. "Okay," she says, hitching up her skirt, "let's get this gong show on the road."

Angela and I file into the tent, where a klezmer band is toodling away in the corner. Our parents are already seated next to my dad's old friend Sally, whose wheelchair is festooned with white bunting and lilacs. She is talking animatedly to my mother, but when we arrive she looks up at us with pale bird eyes.

"Doppel and Ganger," she says, "fancy meeting you here." This is what she's called us for as long as I can remember. She holds out her arms and we each in turn bend down to embrace her.

When we were kids Sally made us mix CDs and gave us diaries with stickers inside that said "Ex Libris." She took us to art galleries and let us watch movies with nudity and violence. She called them "advanced." She'd say "This movie's pretty advanced, so don't get any ideas." She taught us how to put on liquid eyeliner and how to break out of a headlock. Her friends all seemed to be drag queens or women with a lot of tattoos.

As we got older we saw Sally less. I don't know if this had to do with her having MS or something else. Knowing my dad I assumed something else. To the wedding she is wearing brown high-waisted Katharine Hepburn pants, a white blouse, and a vest that matched the pants. Her hair is short brown with a band of grey around the sideburns and bangs, and her ears are pierced with small diamond studs. Around her neck is a chain whose point disappears below the vee of her blouse, but I know for a fact it holds a small gold double-headed axe. I had noticed it as a kid, swinging as she picked us up or leaned forward over a hand of gin rummy. Dad called it The Old Battle Axe. She once told me its true name: Labrys. I didn't know what it meant, then.

Lately she's been experimenting with homeopathic healing, reiki. She tells my dad she's really into vibrations.

"What's reiki?" I ask.

"It's an energy thing," she says.

I can understand this. I've seen auras on dogs, stood beside the Hydro-Québec power house at Manic-5 and felt my hair stand on end. Once I rested my head against a vibrating clothes dryer until I puked. I know the things energy can do.

"How does it work?" I say.

"It has to do with energy following lines of your body called meridians," Sally says. She lifts my arm and runs her finger along the inner edge, where the pale winter skin meets the darker summer skin. "This is your heart meridian." A feeling moves past but not through me, like weather.

Angela nudges me and leans over to speak into my ear, but she's drowned out by the klezmer band launching into "Here Comes the Bride," clarinets wailing like they're announcing the end of the world.

After the ceremony Sally asks me and Angela to take her to the floating dock while white-smocked caterers prepare the tent for the reception. "I want to look at the water," she says. We bump over the uneven ground toward the stone pathway, past the receiving line where Jill, Harris, and my aunt and uncle brush family palms.

Angela halts the wheelchair at the top of a bluff, before the stone path that leads down to the dock. The wind rifles our hair for a while and nobody says anything.

Aunt Lydia comes over. She seems to have recovered from her earlier episode; her cheeks are flushed and she holds a lipsticky glass of champagne and a pink-tipped cigarette in the same pink-tipped hand.

"Well cry me a *river*, that was a beautiful ceremony. Those two kids, you could just eat them for breakfast." And she could, too; she has a hungry, wolfish look. She leans on Sally's wheelchair like it's the railing of a ship and pats me on the cheek.

"You girls," she says. "Which one of you is going to be next?"

"Next?" says Angela. Lydia tilts her head and gives her an eyebrow wiggle.

"I heard you have a suitor," she says. Angela looks shocked, then laughs. I think about a small cottage, wisteria vines. Two cats, named Gertrude and Alice.

"Oh. Oh yeah, that," Angela says. "Yeah, we're off to the chapel any day now."

"You won't forget to invite us, will you?"

"Never."

Lydia catches me in her unfocused gaze. "And you, Stacey?" She leans in and winks.

I look out at the lake and want so badly to be flying over it, just buzzing over the still water with my arms outstretched, like God, like an airplane.

"You shouldn't be ashamed of your seks-you-ality," Lydia says. "Your seks-you-ality is a beautiful thing."

"I'm not," I say. Sally is smiling now too.

"You know," says Lydia, "I know the nicest lesbian couple. They live in my co-op. I could introduce you to them sometime."

I look at Angela, but she's barely there, an outline of a girl looking at a lake.

"That's okay," I say.

"There's no reason for you to be alone," Lydia says.

"There are plenty of people like you in the world. You just have to be willing to open yourself up!"

Sally takes my hand and says she's sure I will make some girl very happy someday. And I think she's right but it won't be the one I want.

Back in the tent, our parents are already at the table. Mom is talking to a broad-shouldered man in a polo shirt; instead of the standard alligator it has a tiny gun embroidered over the heart. His hair is sandy and swept back. He has the look of an aging college athlete, with slightly leathery skin that's part handsome and part sad.

"Stacey, this is your second cousin Mitchell. He's a writer, just like you."

"Oh. Hi."

I'm extended a firm manly-man grasp.

"Ah, Stacey. Aunt Abby was just telling me you have a piece coming out in *Sparkle-Pony*. Congratulations. I haven't heard of it, is it affiliated with a university press?"

"Uh. No. It's kind of an independent publication."

"Cool, man, cool. Anywhere you can get your start."

"Mitchell has a book contract with Knopf," Lydia says. "And he hasn't even finished his book!"

Mitchell smiled and waved one hand dismissively. "It's nonfiction," he said, "that's standard for the industry. Not like what Stacey's doing. The literary houses want to see *product*."

"Well I just think you kids are great," Lydia says. "You follow the rainbow."

"To find the horn of plenty," Mitchell says.

"Exactly," says Lydia.

When the food arrives Mom gives it her usual benediction: "It feels good to be eating." Angela cuts her eyes at me and leaves the table, her purse with the test still in it tucked tightly under one arm.

The DJ puts on Bryan Adams and a few couples start slow-dancing. Dad's holding Mom in a close embrace and murmuring into her neck. The gin and tonic she holds in one hand is dribbling onto the back of his suit jacket.

"Come dance, Stacey," Mom says. She detaches from Dad and starts toward me, swaying side to side and snapping her fingers like some kind of beatnik chimpanzee. She grabs my forearms and tries to lift me out of the chair. I make myself as heavy as possible without looking like I'm doing anything.

"Oh come *on*," she says, "loosen up." She jiggles my arms, and I think about passive resistance. Mom sighs. "Kids can be such fascists," she announces to the tent at large. I slip away as she begins to twirl like a taffeta hurricane.

There's a very long line outside the portable toilets. While I wait I overhear a couple of the groomsmen talking about their favourite porn star, whose name is Iona Dildo.

"She's off the hook," one of them says.

"Off the hizzle."

"Off the hizzay."

"Fo shizzay."

A door swings open, and Angela staggers out of a stall holding her high heels in one hand. She spies me in line, takes my elbow and steers me away from the portable toilets and outside the tent.

"I have to pee," I say.

"Give me a smoke," she says, ignoring my personal needs for the twenty thousandth time. I dig around in my purse for my pack.

"Mitchell's hot," she says, lips clamped on the filter as

she lights.

"You're serious."

"Don't you think so?"

"He's like *forty*. And he's a pretentious twatbag."

"He's thirty-two. And he is not."

"He was making fun of Lydia to her face."

"He was teasing her, *gently*. If she's too dumb to catch on, that's not his fault. Anyway he's an intellectual."

"An intellectual twatbag."

"I'd still do him," she says.

"Do I need to remind you that he's your cousin?"

"So? That didn't stop Bubbe and Zaide."

She has a point. Our grandparents were in fact distantly related. Slim pickings on the shtetl.

"Talk to the hand," I say.

"Tell me you didn't just say that." She turns and walks toward the path leading down to the floating dock, her heels sinking into the wet grass. The melody of "Hava Nagila" floats over the trees and I can faintly hear Jill shrieking as she and Harris and their chairs are hoisted into the air. I think about a baby that looks half like Henry and half like Angela, and therefore half like me. The idea is both compelling and nauseating.

Angela stops suddenly and I almost bump into her. "Give me another smoke," she says.

"Why, are you smoking for two now?"

She gives me a condescending smile and holds out her hand. I grab it and we skid down the gravelly path together and walk out onto the dock.

There is a certain kind of vertigo that comes from looking into deep clear water. Angela sits on the edge of the dock and as I look past her into the copper depths my eyes begin to water. I once climbed a fire escape with Henry and Angela, trying to get to the roof of an abandoned theatre on Parc Avenue. Henry went first, then me, and Angela bringing up the rear. The iron fire escape was bouncing around like something from a 1940s cartoon, jiggling in 4/4 time, and my throat started getting sticky and my eyes watered and about halfway up I just froze solid, with one foot up and my hands in fists around the railings.

"What's the matter," said Henry, "are you afraid of heights?"

"She's afraid of gravity," Angela said. She offered to carry me, and I said no, that wouldn't make a difference, and then she offered to let me carry her, and I said "What if I carry you and you carry me, then we both get a free ride," and then Henry shouted down from the roof, "Get an effing room already guys."

It's the way a rock sticking out of the water looks like a rock, but when you look down you see you're clinging to the tip of a mountain. You count to three, and then you let go.

Now Angela slips off the edge of the dock, into that big empty that somehow holds her and ferries her along, her dress pocketing with air as she breaststrokes through the muscular water. Her back and shoulders glinting.

One.

Two.

Three.

Go.

Sweet Affliction

All the nurses' names end in *nda*: Rhonda, Randa, Amanda, Linda, Little Linda, Panda. No, I made that up. No one is named Panda, though one of Rhonda's tunics is patterned with little pyjama-clad bears. Is *tunic* the right word? Probably not—it's too close to *panic*, which is not encouraged in the ward. People do anyway, but quietly.

"Look," says Doc B. "What I'm telling you doesn't have to be the end of the world. You should think of it rather as an opportunity for personal growth."

Well, I think, *aha. Now we are getting somewhere.*

"*An Opportunity for Growth!*" was, funnily, also the title of the informational pamphlet that came through my mail slot just a few days after the BGD chemical plant opened, a few blocks down from my house. It pictured a spry fellow who was either a blob of soft serve ice cream or a frozen waterfall, with bandy legs, white gloves and a top hat. *Hi, I'm B.B. Begood, and I'm the Newest Addition to Your Neighbourhood! I am looking forward to moving into the Future with You!* These words, speech-bubbled, came out of his mouth. Well, I really believe in the power of coincidences.

They are the universe's way of saying *Hey sister, you're on the right track! Keep on trucking, somebody up there likes you!* And so on. So when Doc B gave me the speech about Metastasis and Prognosis Poor and Recovery Unlikely, not to mention the Opportunity For Growth, it seemed like a sign. Not like a traffic sign, not big and sharp-edged and full of neon warnings. More like a subtle gesture, a twitch in an eyelid or at the corner of your friend's mouth when you ask her how's she feeling, so subtle you barely notice, so subtle even *she* barely notices. And it means this: *You have no idea, but something important is going on here and you are a small but fundamental part of it. Have faith. Hold on.* Or something like that.

BGDs, I learned from the pamphlet, are manufactured molecules that are used primarily in the making of industrial degreasing fluid. *Helping the Wheels of Industry Turn*, as the pamphlet says. Think of it: something that never existed before has been created in the interest of progress, in making things go smoothly and without interruption. If they made BGDs for my life, I would be the first in line.

A documentary filmmaker has been nagging me, emailing and sometimes even showing up at the ward, where Randa or Linda have to shoo her away like a stray dog. She wants to interview me for a "new project" she's working on; something about the environment and corporate accountability, toxic groundwater, the bloom in my bloodstream— all are related. Which, you know, I wholeheartedly believe. But every time I read one of her cheerfully threatening pleas, I get a case of the squirmies. Maybe it's her evident distaste for punctuation and capital letters: *believe me this is the only way we can raise awareness of what they're doing to people like you monsters every last one.* But it's more than that. How can I explain to her that the monsters are all in her head?

Abby, the woman who shares my room, wants me to do it. "Make those bastards pay for what they did to you," she tells me. Because of her nose tube, *make* sounds like *bake*. I understand her bitterness. If only she could know for sure that she was a part of something bigger, the way I do. I keep telling her she's missing the forest for the trees, and she keeps rolling her eyes and grumbling into the latest issue of *Mother Jones.* She thinks I'm a wimp, but maybe she's really jealous of the changes I'm going through. Some people have no concept of the importance of growth.

Rhonda comes in to change Abby's tube. "Oh dear, will I be able to play the piano when all this is over?" I say. It's this little routine we have.

"You gals," Rhonda smiles. She calls me pet names that sound violent but are actually full of affection: a cut-up, a caution, the living end. I think Abby finds our relationship alarming.

The wooded area at the end of the street where I used to live, before I ended up here with Abby, was once a landfill. *Landfill* is a much better word than *junkyard* or *garbage dump*—it sounds so purposeful, like hair gel or cake icing. And the land being filled was the wooded area where I would walk Cocoa Beans. Once enough used diapers and Pop Top Puppies and laptop batteries and torn pantyhose had been recruited, grass was laid over the pile like thick green linoleum, and regularly spaced trees planted on top—Siberian elm, chosen for its ability to grow quickly and in poor soil. And that was my next-door neighbour: the trees, lined up like doormen. Until the plant moved in. Things are always moving in and expanding, the new crowding out the old. Which is pretty much the situation in my uterus at the moment, as Doc B tells me.

"Well Doc," I say, "I guess you know what you're talking about, you are on the right end of the catheter, ha ha!"

On TV the other day there was a story about a man who had a genetic defect that was slowly turning him into a tree. "We do not know exactly why these things occur," said the host, a comforting David Attenborough type, "but we can say for certain that each incidence pushes the species toward greater understanding." Amen, I think.

Incidentally, I believe that when you die, among other things, you get to see the Log Book. The Log Book keeps track of everything, absolutely everything, in the universe, with strict numerical accuracy. How much money you spent on presents for relatives who didn't like you. The total volume, in litres, of lime rickeys you drank. How many people thought about you while they yanked off. And so on.

The documentary filmmaker, a jean-jacketed woman with a silver crescent in her nose, shows me clips from her body of work, to try to convince me to "share my story." A man, a union organizer for a coal mine, stares past the camera and speaks in a flat voice about The System, which is apparently very hard to beat. There are shots of a wasted moon-like landscape, a crumbling bungalow, a man lifting his shirt to show a scar from a bullet that grazed him on a picket line. At the end, a line of text appears on the screen, severe block letters in cinnabar red: CORPORATE ACCOUNTABILITY NOW! "Isn't it a little, you know, grim?" I say. "It could use a bit more pizzazz. How about, like, a dancing cartoon miner's pick? It could be singing that song, the one that goes *ya load sixteen tons, and whaddaya get...*" I sing in a gravelly voice and do jazzy hand gestures like Liza Minnelli in *Cabaret*. The filmmaker narrows her eyes at me like she's checking how I will look in widescreen.

"Corporate accountability isn't about pizzazz," she says. "It's about—"

"Yeah, I know," I say. "Growth."

When the BGD plant first started posting its *Opportunity For Growth!* signs in the wooded area at the end of my street, there were all sorts of protests. Women who looked like the filmmaker except with bigger and more colourful patches on their jeans and men with beards that made them look like perverted old codgers way before their time held homemade signs with slogans like BEGOOD? NO GOOD! and NOT IN MY FORMER LANDFILL. One, surely a relic from causes past, read ASBESTOS? ASWORSTOS! I don't know where they came from—they sure weren't from around here. At the end of the day, a miniature school bus came and they all piled into it and drove away, leaving their picket signs and stubs of hand-rolled cigarettes scattered on the ground. Later, while I was walking Cocoa Beans around the block, I saw that someone, probably the Johansson kids, had arranged the sign sticks on the ground in such a way that they spelt out a dirty word. I bent over and moved a couple of the sticks. AUNT. Much better.

That's when I noticed another woman in the wooded area. She was muttering to herself and tossing the protestors' cast-off recycled paper coffee cups into an orange garbage bag. She was about my age, petite, dressed in a puffy insulated coat that made her look like the Michelin Man. "You don't have to do that," I said. She looked up at me, startled.

"If I don't, who will?"

"No," I said, "I meant talk to yourself like that. You could talk to me instead."

And she smiled. "You live around here?"

"Yep. You?"

"Moving in this July."

"Well," I said, "welcome to the neighbourhood!" Cocoa Beans trotted up and dropped a sandwich wrapper with the words GUTLESS WONDER printed on it in front of her. "What a pain in the keister," I said.

"Yeah. But they're not bad kids. They just don't understand that there are bigger things than them. God knows I didn't, at that age."

"You are so right," I said. "About the bigger things, I mean."

"I'm glad you understand," she said. "Like, all *this*—" she gestured at the wooded area in a non-specific way. "All this once would have been considered unnatural, freakish. But we adapt, we develop a new concept of normal. And we evolve, move forward."

"Into the future," I say.

"Exactly."

Some of the trees were showing signs of disease—pulpy orange thatches on the bark and weird noxious bulges that made me think of acne. "Look," I said to the woman, pointing. "Get this tree an Oxy Pad." And she laughed like I hadn't heard in ages, before or since.

"You are something else," she said.

When the B.B. Begood informational pamphlet came a few months later, I noticed a photo in the bottom right-hand corner. *Shyla Cervenka, General Manager and CEO*. It was the woman from the woods. The Michelin Lady. Well, I thought, good for her.

Today I have a meeting with Grace Showalter. Grace is a Legacy Coach. That is, she helps people figure out how to influence future generations through their stuff. Assets, investments, furniture, artwork, house. Since I have no offspring, my legacy can do all kinds of good for all kinds of people. Grace sits on the edge of my bed holding a very nice leather-bound binder. She is a pleasantly filled-out woman with what they used to call legs that go all the way up.

"I have a few ideas to run by you," she says. "How about KancerKids? They have some really great programs, like FinalFantasy, where you get to—"

"No," I say. "No kids' stuff."

"Hmm, well then, what do you think of Womb For More? They work with survivors of uterine, um, trauma. It might be appropriate."

"Why?" I ask.

"Well, because of, you know—"

"Gosh," I say, "isn't there something with more of a, what do I mean, positive outlook?" Grace frowns at her binder. "Maybe we need to move away from the not-for-profit sector."

"I wholeheartedly agree."

I will tell you about my other legacy, which probably no one will receive. It's a collection of positive adjectives. Incredible, great, awesome, fantastic. Most of them come from *Reader's Digest* and are all-purpose. Some are from women's magazines, and others I picked up from music videos and the internet. Some of them I'm less sure about: wicked, sextastic, sweet, bootylicious, rad. The thing about each of these adjectives is that when applied to the noun *pain* they both retain their original sense and create a whole new meaning. Incredible pain. Wicked pain. Awesome agony. Bootylicious suffering. Sweet affliction.

The filmmaker kneels on the edge of my bed, balancing her video camera on one shoulder. A skinny man hovers a boom mike on a long pole over my head while Abby tries to keep out of the way of its other end, which is jabbing dangerously close to her glucose bag.

"How long ago did you receive the diagnosis?" The filmmaker's voice is calmly inquisitive.

I breathe in. "That video camera—did you know it comes from dinosaurs?"

"Sorry?"

"Dinosaurs. Fossil fuels come from the decayed bodies of dinosaurs, oil products are dead animals from a billion years ago. See?" I point to Abby's pink plastic hairbrush. "Triceratops. The tubes coming out of our bodies, Abby's and mine—brontosaurus. The sound guy's vinyl pants..."

"Lemme guess," the filmmaker says. "T. Rex?"

"Actually," he says, "these are genuine leather."

I take another breath. "Anyway. The dinosaurs couldn't adapt, so they died, but they're still with us, driving our cars and making our records and whatnot. Human beings probably won't adapt either. But," I sit up in bed and try to look prophetic, "at least we can *try*."

I just received the paperwork for the Foundation for the Advancement of the Human Animal from Grace Showalter, who thoughtfully left it on the night table while she thought I was sleeping. In fact I was in a drug-induced stupor, but how was she to know the difference? Sometimes I'm not sure I do. It's going to be a small foundation, funding research on environmental factors in physical evolution of the human species. Like B.B. Begood, like the tree man, like the dinosaurs, I am all about moving forward into the future. I push the paper back into its manila envelope and inhale the gluey smell of the seal. I close my eyes. It's been a long day.

Fifty-two miles of floors mopped. Two car accidents. Seventy hours watching movie stars kiss. Three thousand and seventy-seven styrofoam cups. Three people who called me Darling. Thirteen funerals. And so on.

Moving Day

The moving vans are the first sound you hear. Other days there are garbage trucks, recycling trucks, the *tang tang tang* of the knife sharpener's orange van. But today the moving vans unite the city with their hum: Lynnie asleep on her Therm-a-Rest, Mme Bruges-Robineau snoring under a down-filled duvet, the Love&Squalour House kids rotating on futons, Christophe already awake, having packed nothing, nervously eyeing his alarm clock, which is white and smooth like a Scotch mint. A young mayoral aide doing a sun salutation on bare hardwood, a truck driver clutching a styrofoam coffee cup. Outside their windows vans squat end to end, sniffing each others' tailpipes, already gridlocked, and the sun barely up. Signs across the city, at every major intersection, read OFFICIAL MOVING DAY: NO PARKING. JULY 1ST ONLY.

Moving Day! Half civic crisis and half civic holiday. A festival of exhaust, sweat, lifting, garbage, boxes, masking tape, primer, longing and anticipation. Goodbye to low ceilings, dribbling water pressure, parquet flooring that was spaghetti-stained before you were born. Hello to a whole new bracket of problems, as yet unknown. A new apartment is like a new lover: the inevitability of disappointment understood only with the dry and logical part of the mind, the rest soaked with lust and thrilling at the prospect of the new! Each shortcoming a delight, a foible to be treasured, appreciated, loved! A chance to assess potential, scout necessary renovations, roll up the sleeves! The heart thumps at the discovery of an infestation of mould in the bathroom, a crack in a weight-bearing wall. Tenants sing as they mix buckets of plaster and pour one part bleach to three parts water, the tunes blending in the alleyways and giving each neighbourhood its distinctive feel.

This joyful, fluttering phase lasts three to five months. After that it starts to get old. New problems arise before old ones have fully abated; what once seemed like character is revealed to be dinge. The clever solutions you devised, the ways of making do, are proven shabby and superficial. Depression and despair creep in, more or less in sync with the mildew. But by then, twelve months have passed, and it's time to move again!

Mme Bruges-Robineau hefts the last of her late husband's Harvard Classics into the Easthill Nuisance Tube. She dusts off her hands and watches the books flutter into the vacuum-sealed tunnel, where they will merge with the waste of every other citizen of Easthill and tumble their way downhill into a dumpster in the centre of St. Louis-Cyr, which the kids of working-class families will pick through, looking for discarded video games that some rich child has outgrown. As a homeowner, Mme Bruges-Robineau isn't obliged to participate in Moving Day, but she likes to make a symbolic gesture each year, casting off some long-hoarded item in solidarity with the tenants. She wonders if anyone in St. Louis-Cyr, maybe the vitamin-deficient child of a factory labourer, will look through her husband's collection of canonic fiction and find something of value.

Alex, Sally, J-J-J-Jenny, and The Skills sit on the curb, pulling at tallboys concealed in paper bags. Sally's homemade bike trailer, The Proletariat Chariot, idles, waiting to receive a load of discarded furniture culled from alleyways and curbs. Moving Day will provide them with enough "obtainium" to furnish their apartment. The rest will be sanded, repainted, hand-stencilled, and sold on consignment in one of the new boutiques on Rue Notre-Dame. For now they wait, fanning themselves with newspapers, huffing exhaust and stirred-up dust from the vans.

There's a point at which packing becomes not a material question but an existential one. Lynnie sits on the Persian rug in the middle of the floor, the only thing left unboxed in her apartment, and stares at a pink milk crate marked "mixtapes." God help us. Fifteen years of relationships, friendships, road trips, trades and theme parties, and what she has is this—a crate full of cassettes she doesn't even own a player for. Half the labels on them have either smudged or peeled off, and others have been taped over, making the labels pointless.

She pulls out one marked *who will police the police, and who's gonna make up the make-up artist*, and perches it on her nose like a pair of antique spectacles. The question is, will she be one of those people who hoards things like mixtapes just in case? For some unmet, barely fathomable progeny? Lynnie imagines herself explaining the phenomenon to a blurry group of children gathered around a hearth. "So this was how people in the olden days would tell each other they were special?" one would ask. "Yes," Lynnie would answer, "but you had to be careful. You couldn't be too obvious about it." "Why not?" another would pipe up, a girl with chestnut ringlets who looked a lot like Lynnie's sister. "Well," Lynnie would tell her, "let's pretend that Uncle Sebastien gave me a tape where the first song is the one by The Brooks, the one that goes *Hey hey baby you're just a little girl, hey hey baby c'mon and rule my world.* Does that make Seb a cool guy or a douchebag?" And together all the little children would chorus "DOUCHEBAG!"

No, Lynnie can't really believe in that as a reason for holding on to the tapes. But how can she throw them out? She sighs. With a sharp flick of the wrist she snaps the tape back into the crate.

She pulls out a letter from her jeans pocket and reads it again, hoping that through some miracle the words have rearranged themselves. *We regret to inform you that no vacancy is currently available... Please rest assured that the Bureau is working to change this unfortunate situation... Until further notice...* Written on city letterhead and signed by Mayor Girofle herself. Lynnie licks a finger and rubs it over the signature. The ink doesn't smear. A copy, then. It's just as well.

She looks at her watch. The new tenant will arrive in an hour.

She decides to leave it up to fate. She will leave the pink crate on the curb. Whatever is left by the time she has to go, she will take with her. Let the Obtainium Crew decide what the children of tomorrow will know of her life.

A family of four is lounging on the grassy meridian between the northbound and southbound lanes of the expressway.

They have erected a homemade signpost made out of an old coat rack and cardboard, on which is Sharpied *Decarie Island*. The sign is illustrated with a jagged palm tree and a smiling sun wearing wraparound shades, like an orange juice ad. The parents sprawl in lawn chairs, the woman reading the *Journal de Montréal*, while the two kids, boy and girl, sit in the scrub grass and play with beach toys. An elderly beagle squats panting beside the chairs. Behind the kids is a pup tent, and at the far end of the meridian is a portable toilet.

"I promised my family an island vacation," the man says to reporters and curious onlookers. "With the economy the way it is this was all we could afford."

They've been there for five days, but they say they will probably have to leave soon because of the threats from PETA.

"Because of the dog," the woman says. Her skin is crisp-looking and coated in coconut oil. "They think he's being exposed to dangerous levels of carbon monoxide."

Cars on either side of the meridian stretch to the horizon.

Christophe isn't going anywhere. That's what he tells the new tenants—an East Indian family migrating south from St. Amande—as well as the neighbours, the landlord, Mayor Girofle's team of aides and various media representatives.

"I worked for years to afford the rent on this place. Do you know how many legal briefs that is? A million. Roughly. And all I wanted was this. High ceilings, recently-sanded hardwood floors, stainless steel bathroom fixtures. Is that too much to ask?" He points to a heavy-looking hammered-brass doorknob. "Look. I ordered those myself from a manufacturer in Belgium. Going out of business sale. Last of their kind. Watched a video, learned how to install them myself. And for what? To pass it on to... to... a family of immigrants—no offense, I'm sure you're very nice—who haven't even heard of Charles and Ray Eames?" Christophe lifts a hand to his forehead and covers one eye, picturing a statue of a many-armed god, or some multicoloured prayer flags, in the window nook where his 1956 recliner sits.

One of Girofle's aides starts to hum the Moving Day anthem, a soothing patriotic ditty. In situations like this he is meant to cite the Moving Day bylaws as well as the Moving Day poem, composed by the poet-in-residence at the Richler library, but he feels personally that music is the more effective medium for calming nerves and inspiring tenants to perform their duty. This time, though, it only makes the outgoing tenant stand his ground more firmly, while the incomers crowd the doorway, equally obstinate.

"I beg your pardon," says the mother of the family. She is dressed in a puffy powder-blue coat, despite the heat. "I don't know what they taught you in this country, but that was never an Eames chair."

Christophe keeps his hand over his eye and stares at her in mono. "I'm sorry?"

"Look at how he looks at me," the woman goes on. "It's as though a dog has spoken. Typical Pepsi racist. Take your Ikea nonsense and get out of my house."

A small muscle at the corner of Christophe's mouth begins to twitch. "I will ignore that last remark," he says, "if you will concede that you would not know an Eames chair if it walked up and asked you the time of day."

The woman crosses her arms and lifts her chin. "Your rear end I wouldn't," she says. Her two children look at each other and giggle, while several camera flashes go off.

"Moving Day is an opportunity for growth!" the aide says. "A citizen embraces Moving Day like a child greeting the new day, like a morning peach, like a gazelle on the Serengeti, stretching its antlers to the sun—"

"You be quiet," the woman says. The aide bows his head to his clipboard.

"Look," Christophe says, "forget the chair. The point is that—" What is the point, actually? For a second he can't recall. He scratches at the nape of his neck and stares out the window. Momentarily he imagines he is at the returns desk of a very large department store, arguing with a clerk over an espresso maker that was already broken when he removed it from its box. Then the lineup of trucks, crawling down the street an inch per minute, triggers his memory.

"I just think," he says, "I mean, is this really necessary?" As soon as the word leaves his mouth he knows the argument is over.

"Necessary?" says another aide, this one a young woman with curly black hair. "Moving Day is not about necessary. It's a matter of civic duty, an expression of love for your city. What is necessary? By whose standards? Do we need rainbows to live? Shadows? Fingernails? And yet, can we imagine life without them?"

She's pretty good, Christophe thinks, and this momentary distraction allows the new tenant to push past him into the living room proper and throw down her suitcase with a loud leathery thump.

It is an Eames chair, Christophe knows it, but the idea is becoming more and more abstract, as though the chair's provenance rested on the goodwill of the neighbourhood, the aides, the media, and not a seal burned into the leather on the chair's underside. He will have to believe harder, next time.

When Lynnie brings the next load of junk out to the curb she sees what she expected to see—a young woman in a neon green tank top and sturdy overalls, coarse black hair pulled into a rat's tail, picking through the tapes in her crate. Lynnie clears her throat, almost involuntarily.

"Hey," says the young woman, looking up. "Are these yours?"

"Yup," says Lynnie.

"You have, like, every Tutti Fervour album ever."

"True fan," says Lynnie, setting down a box of chipped mugs and dishes next to the crate.

"I haven't listened to her in ages," says the woman. "She rules. Why are you throwing them out?"

"Well..." says Lynnie. The answer to this seems so complicated she doesn't know where to begin.

"Moving Day, right?" says the woman.

"Yeah."

"And you didn't want to bring them to your new place?"

"I don't have a new place."

The woman considers this. "That sucks," she says.

"Big time," says Lynnie.

The woman tilts her head and looks into the sun for a moment. Then she looks back at Lynnie, still squinting. "What's your name?"

"Lynnie," says Lynnie.

"Sally," says Sally. "Maybe I can help."

Philippe pops the clutch and shifts to second gear. He hears that sound again, the one like grinding teeth, coming from somewhere in the vicinity of what would be his truck's kidneys if his truck had a digestive tract like a person, which he isn't entirely convinced it doesn't. Come on, baby, not today. Any day but today. A good mover like Philippe can pull down enough cash on Moving Day to coast through the rest of the summer like a CEO, but not if his truck craps out on him.

The radio is playing an odd assortment of military music and sixties bubble gum; he switches to the community station in time to hear the end of a report on stand-offs between tenants and mayoral aides. The aides were reportedly using tactics like stinkbombs and high-decibel techno to clear out some especially residual residents. Not something for the city brochures, if you ask Philippe. The youthful journalist claims the newest batch of aides have been trained at the same military institution as certain guards at a notorious terrorist detention camp, but that seems like a bit much for his money.

Philippe thinks back to the conversation with the badger-faced man he had driven home from The Miracle. Easy money, the badger-face had promised. How often you use this truck anyway? Once a month? You know what this is? This is valuable real estate, is what this is. The words coming to Philippe on waves of vodka tonic. Greasy words from a greasy man.

He checks his GPS and pulls up a half-block before his first pickup. The truck is directly underneath an overpass at the mouth of St. Louis-Cyr. He slides out and goes around to the back, pops the latch and hoists the metal door.

"All right," he says, "time's up. Godspeed and all that."

The family inside turns and blinks at him, all in unison, like a family of owls. They have a little cooking fire going in there, which is not according to Hoyle but he turns a blind eye sometimes, not like other movers he could name, bounty hunters et cetera who are all too eager to turn a paperless family in. They're so coated in soot and grime it's hard to tell what they are.

"C'mon," he says, "beat it. I got to move a family of four in ten minutes. Get." Philippe is patient as the next guy, but honestly. A month they'd been living in there. You'd think they'd be on fire to get out. Plus he has to admit that overpass is grinding his nerves like anything. The badger-faced man isn't paying him nearly enough for this.

The little girl in the back of the truck shows him all ten of her fingers. She closes her fists, then opens them, and then once again. Thirty days.

"Yeah," he says. "Yeah yeah yeah."

The St. Louis-Cyr dumpster is unusually brimming, so Alex has to watch his footing as he picks his way through the metal bin. He wears gardening gloves from the dollar store and a purple bandana over his nose and mouth. The dumpster is the size of a boxcar—in fact, the graffiti on the side suggests it *was* a boxcar, before being relegated to an empty lot below an overpass, ready to receive the city's assorted waste. The Skills surmises that some of the tags originated in the Pacific Northwest, while others are clearly Chicago-style.

Sally points to an airbrushed drawing of a cat on a skateboard on the dumpster's side, done in migraine-yellow and seasick-pink. "I know that," she says. "That's Miladee's work. She was one of the original members of the Boston Ladies' Auxiliary Bomb Squad."

"And?" Alex says, examining the spine of a paperback book. Dickens's *David Copperfield*, a Harvard Classics edition. He starts to put it in his backpack, then takes it out again.

"And she fell under a boxcar, couple years back. Lost a leg. They say she painted a huge mural on the wall of the physio clinic, then disappeared."

"Spooky," he says. He opens the book, reads the *Ex Libris* on the flyleaf. A feeling like a cold finger on his neck ripples through him, and he shivers in the heat.

"What," says Sally.

"Nothing," says Alex. "Allergies." He tosses the book to The Skills, saying "Put it in the pile for Welch's."

"Here it comes!" says J-J-J-Jenny. And they all hear it: the steady faraway rumble accompanied by a high-pitched whistling, a forced-air sound. Then the tube above Alex's head begins to vibrate, and the rumble becomes a clanging. Alex leaps to a corner of the boxcar, crouches and covers his head. The lid of the tube flings open with a roar and a rush of stale air, and a clot of material—wood, cloth, paper, cushions, books—whumps out and crashes onto the pile. The sides of the boxcar shudder, and go still. Alex stands up, coughing, as dust particles, feathers and bits of pink fluff settle around him. His shirt is stuck all over with tiny Styrofoam balls.

"Whoa," says Sally. "Big day." She hoists herself up one side of the dumpster, and, taking Alex's hand, swings one leg then the other onto the refuse heap. She squats gingerly and starts picking her way through a collapsed stack of DVDs. The smell from the dumpster is heat and dust more than animal or vegetable. It reminds her maybe of factories, places where things get made, where grease and sweat keep everything turning. She closes her eyes.

A crowd on foot moves through the traffic jam in the Old Port. They carry flags and hand-held signs. They beat drums and play tin flutes and someone periodically pumps a few resonant belches from a tuba. Some are dressed all in black, some wear fluorescent legwarmers and neon tunics and some just look regular. Cars honk as they pass, in frustration or solidarity, each honk eliciting a corresponding outburst of cheers from the crowd, regardless of the driver's intent. The crowd is moving toward the mayor's office in the yearly protest against Moving Day.

Christophe steps quickly through the centre of the crowd. He can't quite get a comfortable grip on the sign he's holding. First his right and then his left arm tires, and when he uses both hands his shoulders start acting up. He tries resting the wooden beam of the sign against one shoulder like a rifle, but the cardboard corners keep getting tangled up in the long dreadlocks of the girl walking beside him.

"Sorry," he says.

"No worries," she replies.

He lowers the sign and tries to use it as a walking stick. The crowd is beginning to chant.

"TENANTS UNITE, KEEP UP THE FIGHT"

"À QUI LES DOMICILES? À NOUS LES DOMICILES!"

"HELL NO, WE WON'T PACK"

As the crowd approaches the mayor's office the drumming increases in volume and speed, and the chants break down into a general din of shouts and cheers. Someone is blowing a whistle right next to Christophe's ear. He reaches a finger into the collar of his shirt. It's damp in there, and sticky. He wishes he had worn something lighter than the collared shirt and sweater-vest he had on when leaving the house, but most of his clothes had been hastily packed away and there was no time.

A slender young man in a pink shirt and purple bandanna hands him a flyer for a Moving Day party at some dumpy loft in St. Louis-Cyr. He thanks the man and folds it into his pocket.

Outside the mayor's office an area is cordoned off with police tape. Riot police surround the Designated Self-Expression Zone, looking like clunky toys with their shields and helmets. The crowd, moving single-minded as a flock, sidesteps the DSEZ and continues on down the block. Above their heads, a couple of teenage girls stand on the balcony of a glass and steel condominium, banging pots and pans and waving at the crowd. Some people cheer and throw fists in the air. The woman next to Christophe pulls down her bandana.

"Yuppies!" she shouts. "Homeowner scum-spawn! If you're so down why aren't you down here!" The girls smile and wave. One of them blows bubbles with a red plastic wand.

The sun glints off a corner of the building and Christophe looks away. He thinks about the boxes of clothes and books and dishes piled in the back seat of his car, parked outside his old apartment. He had nowhere to put the Eames chair and so he left it next to the car, with a neatly lettered sign on it reading BEDBUGS. That ought to discourage the salvage crews. By now the new family has probably finished cleaning all traces of him from the light switches, the bathroom mirror, the doorjambs: all those places where bits of him have collected and smeared. The house will be crisp and foreign-smelling.

The crowd has stopped moving now. The woman with the dreadlocks is doing a strange, herky-jerky dance, all elbows and knees, shaking her head from side to side and lifting and dropping her heavy work boots. A man shimmies to the top of a traffic sign, pulls off his T-shirt one-handed and waves it like a flag. Christophe blanches at the sight of his puffy nipples and fungus-white torso, but he envies the man's bareness. He untucks his shirt and smiles tightly at the woman, who gives him a friendly if slint-eyed look in return. Probably she wonders if he's undercover.

"Looks like they've got us surrounded," the woman says, pointing her chin at the riot police.

"Yeah," Christophe agrees, heartened by her use of *us* and *them*, his inclusion in the crowd's animal body. He feels drawn in, as to a warm bath or a hug. The woman shrugs, opening and lifting her arms in a gesture that is at once resigned and resolute. She rolls her eyes and does a nifty soft-shoe, hands gripping an invisible cane. Christophe watches her until she disappears between a grey-haired woman and a papier mâché effigy of the mayor. A few moments later, he feels the first sting of the water cannon on the back of his head.

When Lynnie arrives at Sally's place the first thing she sees is a grey cat curled up in a handsome leather recliner. Sally lifts the cat, who mewls in protest, and flops down into the chair. "Ahhh," she says, "another day, another dollar."

"Nice chair," says Lynnie.

"I know, right? It's real. I mean..." Sally clears her throat. "I mean it's a real designer chair. Fifties minimalism. I could get good money for it on eBay, but I don't know." She wiggles her ass, and the chair moans a bit, like a dreaming animal. "I kind of love it."

"Where should I put this?" Lynnie says, lifting the box she's holding.

"Oh. The room is on the other side of the kitchen. The

housemates are still out scavenging, so make yourself at home. One of our friends was supposed to take it last week, but he decided to spend the summer studying taxidermy in the Yukon, so..." Sally's voice fades out as Lynnie moves through the hallway.

On one wall of the kitchen someone has spraypainted *Love & Squalour* in baby-blue cursive. Lynnie examines the fridge door, as she always does in an unfamiliar home. Like a beach, all sorts of detritus washes up there, and it can tell you what kind of environment you're in. There are hand-drawn and Letraset fliers for bands with names like Performance Anxiety and East Infection, expired coupons for Dairy Queen, a program grid for the local community radio station, blurry shots of kids jammed four and five to a photobooth. There is a FREE TIBET bumper sticker; the words "with every purchase" are Sharpied beneath.

"So how come you guys didn't have to move?" Lynnie calls over the kitchen's cavernous space. "Someone who lives here owns the place?"

"Nah," says Sally, "we squat. Someone had a lease here, once, but..." She trails off. "I guess we're just waiting around for someone to notice us, and hoping they don't."

"I know what you mean," Lynnie says, though she doesn't.

"Let me show you around," says Sally. She takes Lynnie through a back garden (tomatoes and peppers in buckets, pole beans and sweet peas climbing homemade trellises, herbs for cooking and medicine); a bathroom converted to a darkroom and silkscreen wash station; a "chill-out room" full of half-decomposed bikes and tools; and the workshop, where furniture in various stages of strip, repair and paint sits on thick greasy carpets of newspaper. The room reeks of varnish. Lynnie recalls someone passing her a tiny bottle of amyl nitrate on a dance floor and instructing her to sniff: the sick-sweet piercing of her nasal cavity, the nauseated sense of wellbeing, and the headache. She feels a mild high just standing in the doorway.

"I know, it stinks," Sally says. "Alex started building a ventilation system but he kind of got distracted. Your room is pretty far away, but if it's a problem…"

Sally has a formal way of fading out her sentences, as though she has no intention of ever finishing them.

"It isn't," Lynnie says.

From one channel to the next, the news is the same. Riots, mass arrests, angry people shouting in the streets. Every year, every channel, the same stream of images like some kind of ritual. The same burning moving van appears over and over, as though it's the new emblem for current affairs. The same tearful driver speaks to the off-camera reporter, the same words, the same gesture of hopelessness and frustration. Mme Bruges-Robineau can't hear the words, but she understands the gist. Her fingers are slick and greasy with popcorn butter, and she licks them distractedly. The remote too is becoming shiny, deposits of saturated fat coagulating around the buttons, but she restrains herself from sucking one end of it like a Fudgesicle.

She flips the channel, then quickly flips it back. She unmutes the voices.

"—our only means of democratic expression at this point," a young man says. He is being interviewed in front of one of the glass buildings of the Old Port that are like mirrored sunglasses. At the bottom of the screen his name appears, Alex Prole ("Ha," thinks Madame, "that's a good one,") followed by his affiliation, an acronym for a tenants' association. He is tall and narrow, wearing a faded pink shirt and a purple bandanna around his neck. It strikes Madame that in spite of all predictions he now looks more like her than like his father. Alex answers a few more questions and then the news shifts to another part of town, a suburb where two families shout at each other as aides and neighbours look on. Madame surfs for a few minutes, hoping to see the clip of Alex again, but all she can find is the burning moving van, commercials, and, now that the sun is down, the usual assortment of pay-per-view shills.

She thinks about writing a cheque to Alex's housing association, what was it called? He wouldn't accept money from her personally, she knows that, having already received an envelope containing a torn-up cheque and a photocopied pamphlet about Marxism, but maybe she can make a donation to his group. He won't be able to refuse that. She goes looking for her purse, stops to pet the cat. She's already forgotten the name.

Last Man Standing

I had lived in the apartment for about a month when there was a knock on the door.

"You probably shouldn't answer that," my roommate said. But I was halfway there. They would have already heard my footsteps.

At the door was a very short woman in overalls and a blue T-shirt.

"Can I use your phone?" she said. I handed her my cell and pressed my foot down on the cat as he tried to slip out the door.

"Sorry," I said to the woman. She stared at me, saying nothing, holding the phone to her head. She didn't seem to have dialled, but then I was distracted. She shook her head and handed me the phone, looking around nervously. She appeared to be distraught, or high. The cat struggled out of my arms and I went after him again. The woman didn't seem done yet, so I asked her to come inside so I could close the door. She leaned in and spoke into my face.

"My baby," said the woman. "He's hurt. I need to take him to the hospital." She had several teeth missing, and several more were dull gold.

"Do you need me to call you an ambulance?"

"Please," she said, "no ambulance." I couldn't place her accent. "I can't afford the ambulance. Please, sir, my baby is hurt."

"Where's your baby?" I said.

"I need to take him to the hospital. In a cab." She eyed my recording equipment, which was visible through the doorway to my room. It wasn't so fancy, but to a crackhead it would look like Big Rock Candy Mountain.

I clued in.

"Okay," I said. "What's it going to cost me to get you out of my apartment."

She paused for a moment. "Twenty dollars," she said.

I tossed the cat into the bathroom and closed the door. When I came back with the money she was swaying a little and humming to herself.

"All I have is a ten," I said.

She took it and nodded. "I'll bring it back tomorrow." I closed the door on the sound of her shoes tapping down the stairs.

I flipped open the phone and looked through the recent calls. I highlighted the most recent one and pressed the green button. Surprisingly, it connected. I let it go for ten rings and then I snapped the phone shut. My roommate was rolling a joint on the sofa.

"Someone you know?" he said.

"Sure," I said.

The rest of the day passed in a kind of pleasant undulation, like driving down the California coast in a big Cadillac with the radio on, just listening to whatever, with the cliffs on one side and on the other the green and deadly ocean.

Around three in the morning, my phone rang. This usually means either bad news or my cousin Micah is in town.

"Hello," I said.

"You called me," said a man's voice on the other end.

"I don't think so," I said.

"Well someone called me from this number," he said. "Twice."

I thought very hard, forcing my way from sleep. Something about an ambulance and money, mine.

"You owe me ten dollars," I said.

"What? Is this Mario? I fuckin' told you, Mario. I told you. Don't call me at this number."

"This isn't Mario," I said. "But you still owe me ten dollars."

"No fuckin' way," the guy said, but he sounded a bit shaken.

"How's the baby," I said.

"What baby?"

"The baby. The one that had to go to the hospital."

"Is that a threat?" he said.

"Yeah, it's a fuckin' threat," I said, improvising.

"Who the fuck is this?"

"Someone who wants his ten dollars back."

"Listen man, I don't know if you're a friend of Mario's or what the fuck, but you come at me like that, you got me feeling some kind of way. Fuck you."

"No, fuck you," I said. I was getting bored. I clacked the phone shut and went back to sleep. It rang almost immediately, so I set it to silent.

In the morning I opened the phone and listened for the dial tone. Of course there wasn't one. There was no such thing as a dial tone anymore.

I had thirty-three missed calls, all from the mystery

number. There were fourteen messages. The first three were strings of curses. The rest were just a bunch of muffled noises. The guy had probably been pocket-dialling me all night. I lit a cigarette and pressed Delete fourteen times.

My roommate was already on the sofa, playing an N64 he had found in the alley. He tossed me a soda without even looking. He had the radio on, and a woman with a heavy Queb accent was hosting a phone-in show. The theme was "Dog Sweaters: For or Against?"

I twisted the top off the pop bottle, then used a butter knife to pry the plastic circle out from under the cap. Come on, jackpot.

"What does it say?" Brendan asked.

"Please Play Again."

"Well, I would hardly call that playing," he said.

I went downstairs to check the mail. A white eleven-by-fourteen envelope was crammed into the narrow box despite the serious red *Do Not Fold* stamped on it. I carried it back upstairs.

"What's that?" Brendan said.

"My degree," I said. He laughed, and I went into my room.

When I held the envelope up to the window I could vaguely see the Latin words written on it, and below them my name. The cat stood in the doorway, waiting for me to put the envelope down so he could sit on it.

"Are you the most special creature in the universe," I asked.

Probably, he seemed to say.

That evening me, Brendan, and Renaud, the building super, went to The Miracle for a drink. It was the kind of night you know you're going to see people who look like famous people. Renaud ordered a pink frothy drink from a woman with a neck striped from self-tanning. A strange guy sat down next to me and asked if he could have a sip of my beer. He was probably about my age, twenty-eight, but he looked fifty-five.

"Listen, is the night a time, a place, or a thing?" he said.

"It's a noun, that's for sure."

"It's a state of *mind*," Renaud said.

The Miracle didn't have a bar license, so Maryse, the owner, would serve a provisional sort of buffet with the drinks, half a bagel and a sliced-up apple, or a handful of potato chips and some Babybel cheese. Then she'd go to her armchair in the corner and nod off, her turtleneck pulled up over half her face. This time it was a stale tortilla and a bowl of salsa. Maryse shrugged apologetically as she set them down. "The economy," she said, "you know." She was wearing a shirt that said *I'm Kind Of A Big Deal*.

We smoked those cigarettes that come in two sections, smokes and filters. You put them together yourself and save a dollar. We knew a guy who knew a guy who one time opened his pack to find both sections were cigarettes. It was pretty much the most exciting thing to happen that year. In every pack there are always a couple more filters than cigarettes, and we would save them up for the day when we too would be beneficiaries of the universe's generous nature.

I still had the envelope with me. I put it on the table, where it quickly started to look like an Olympic flag. Next to us two young guys were discussing the method of staying out until the very end of the night, when the bar is about to close, at which point you get to take home the drunkest girl there.

"I know that method," one guy said. "It's called 'Last Man Standing.'"

"No it isn't," said his companion. "It's called 'Taking Out the Trash.'"

"Last Man Standing."

"Taking Out the Trash."

Brendan got up to stoke the jukebox. It was playing mostly French tear-jerker songs. I knew what he was going to put on, and I kind of hated him for it. I hated both of us.

On the other side of the room I saw the woman who owed me ten dollars. She was sitting at the bar with a blond man who looked like one of the Norwegians from *Twin Peaks*. I went over and tapped her on the back.

"I know what you're going to say," she said. Her accent was gone.

"How's the baby?" I said.

She laughed. Brendan's song came on—it was The Eagles.

"Do you want to dance?" I said. She smiled and came into my arms. She was taller than I originally thought; her head fit just under my chin.

"I got a degree today," I said. "A master's in political philosophy."

She laughed again. Brendan started to sing along.

Horseman, Pass By

Hall was dying. Alex didn't think he would last the night, so he sat up with him, trying to get him to drink a little, stroking his head and whispering comforting nonsense. Kept everyone out of the sickroom, as he called it, insisting his housemates take off their shoes and turn their music down. Even if Hall made it to morning it wouldn't be long. The tumours were as big as Texas.

It was to be expected, things being what they were, but what was going to happen to Oates?

Alex felt queasy at the thought of Oates' impending aloneness. Like the elderly couple together so long that your partner's face is more familiar than your own, the rats had been together from birth and had no concept of what it meant to be single, unique. Quite likely Hall thought himself to be a white rat and Oates a black, when in fact it was the other way around. Soon Oates would not even have that much; any concept of his own identity would fade with the removal of Hall's body. He would sleep alone in his pile of chips, a fat white comma with no reflection, the last of his kind.

They were five living in the house, seven if you counted

the rats, which no one did except Alex. So five, in a kind of practised and cautiously maintained intimacy. They occupied each others' territory like resistance fighters in a European forest, listening for snapped twigs that signalled coming disaster. They knew each other's routines, the creaking chairs and bedsprings, the toilet flushes and rhythms of dishes by the sink. They knew each others' footsteps, each with their own character.

One fall, when Alex couldn't take it anymore, he moved into a housing complex for deaf students. It would be quiet as a churchyard; he imagined learning to meditate. Of course, there was a serious flaw in his reasoning. Deaf people see no reason not to put up shelves at midnight, to vacuum, to run a few k on a treadmill. The building was a constant clamour of humming, muttering, thunking somethings and clattering other things. "Sometimes they watch TV for the picture," Alex said, "and they have no idea the volume is on full. And you think, I guess I'm going to have to bang on the wall now. But then you realize."

He moved back in a season later, chastened, and with a pair of baby rats he'd rescued from a pet store, who had been destined to be food for an eight-foot python. "Alex Prole's Bourbon Folly," the housemates had called them, though he hadn't been drunk when he bought them, only a little buzzed, a state that was less about intoxication than expansion.

Now he sat with one hand inside the cage, stroking Hall's ears that were even thinner than paper, ears like what you would use to clean a gold ring or something else valuable and easily scratched, while Oates nervously chewed extrusions in the corner. You'd have to say he chewed nervously, because what else could he be feeling, anxiety comprising maybe eighty percent of his emotional range. The cage smelled a bit, it was true, but it was a hearty, musky tang that Alex liked, nothing at all like halitosis. "Yes it is," Sally said. "If it were coming from Sara Bronsky you'd love it," he said accusingly, and she rolled her eyes and gagged, waving around a lit stick of incense like a holy thing.

The only other pet they'd had was a hamster that someone's sister had got tired of. They used it to trim the lawn. Sally would set the top half of the cage on the grass and let the hamster go at it. Every hour or so she'd move the cage over a foot. In a day the lawn would be patchy and the hamster logey and irritable. One day someone stole the hamster, leaving the cage. Who would do such a thing, the housemates wondered. "Stole" was probably a kind guess.

Alex looked up to see Marcus in the doorway, holding two bottles of Cheval Blanc. He tilted one at Alex, who shook his head. Marcus sighed and flicked his bangs out of his face.

"Well, hang in there, buddy."

"When did you start saying 'buddy,'" said Alex. But Marcus had already gone.

Marcus and Alex had known each other since junior high, having bonded over a love of absurdism, read and practised. They met in the after-school improv club, where they discovered a natural rhythm existed between them, a kind of organic Bugs Bunnyish anarchism. While other kids worshipped Nirvana and Skinny Puppy, their master and commander was Samuel Beckett, followed closely by Kafka and Tom Robbins. Like knights of old they were sworn to oppose a common enemy, The Tyranny of the Dull Mind, which covered teachers, parents, Scout leaders, authority figures of all kinds, suck-ups, brown-nosers, teachers' pets, celebrity worshippers, potheads, homecoming kings and queens, organized religion, and the Media, except for a handful of community radio and television shows they enthusiastically endorsed.

One of their favourite games was called Hangman of the Absurd; it was modelled on the original Hangman, with a few minor modifications. All the answers were the sort of phrases one would find in William S. Burroughs, or the beloved Robbins, or nowhere at all. For example: *Sylphs in Small Cars. Pandemonium Pimple Garage. Anarchy Among the Marmosets.* Additionally, when your opponent guessed a wrong letter, instead of a body part you drew whatever you felt like: an ear, a banjo, a porcupine. The game ended when the phrase was filled in or guessed, or the drawing was deemed to be complete. Depending on the length and difficulty of the phrase and the patience of the person doing the drawing, the game could last up to an hour, or the length of their chemistry class.

One day in early fall Marcus went to pick up Alex for the yearly tryouts for the improv team. Alex was sitting against his locker, the hood of his sweatshirt pulled almost over his face. He didn't move. Marcus waited.

"Improv is for brown-nosers," Alex said.

Marcus waited.

"The real possibilities are out there in the streets." He handed Marcus a flyer.

"Radical Cheerleading?"

Alex looked up. "Are you in?"

At first they hung around the back of the demonstrations and marches, but it wasn't long until they were a common sight in the front lines, each holding the end of a banner, or playing timpani and tuba, or taking turns hoisting a political effigy on their shoulders. They had an energy that everyone loved, though to each other they could never resist riffing on the chants, which they agreed sounded boring and fascistic.

"What do we want?"

"Surrealism!"

"When do we want it?"

"Shoehorn!"

They went to different universities, Marcus to the highly ranked Ivy League–ish one where, he joked, his classmates were too privileged to realize how privileged they were. Alex went to the other university, the one promising education "for the real world," with its mosaic of outrageously hip art students, grungy activists and business school fledgling tycoons. They found a five-bedroom two-floor apartment together, with a massive yard in which they planned to grow their own food, build a greenhouse and host weekly bonfires. Three housemates moved in—Sally, J-J-J-Jenny, and Lynnie.

J-J-J-Jenny's stutter was selfish, a way for her to take up three times her share of airtime. An only child, she sang musicals in the shower. Sally was a performance artist and Lynnie was training to be a midwife. Sally stayed the longest, and was the most unaccountably bitter about it. Things you would think were comforting, like watching the kids next door grow up, just made her angry. "It just said *hi* to me," she said once, "and I was here when it was a fucking *tadpole*." She and Alex became close quickly, which Marcus attributed to their shared homosexuality.

Marcus still did theatre, still went to protests, and though he had moved beyond Tom Robbins, he kept his anti-establishment tendencies. He had discovered James

Joyce; his new mantra was *I will not serve*. This he wrote on the inside cover of all his school notebooks, tall and narrow with mottled black and white covers, and he planned to use the money his parents would give him for his next birthday to get a tattoo, *non serviam*, on the inside of his left wrist. He saw himself as a kind of undersea creature, silently floating through the seas of upwardly mobile neolibs and fascist hippies and doctrinaire professors, attached to nothing, absorbing what he needed in order to explode, when the time came, in a spray of ink and radicalism. When would it come, and how would he know it had arrived? He wasn't sure, but he waited with tentacles extended, supple and aware, listening for earthquakes under the seabed.

Alex, meanwhile, had become an ideologue. Or so it seemed to Marcus, who saw his roommate less and less often. When he did, Alex seemed distant and preoccupied; he was starting to get a haggard and fanatical look about the eyes. He communicated mostly by pamphlet—he was in the habit of handing them out to the housemates like the young well-muscled guys Marcus would see on Ste-Catherine, with flyers for clubs with loud names like Boom and Shaker. Protests, demos, manifs, workshops, sit-ins, skillshares, occupations, benefits and benefices—they floated from Alex like dandruff. It wasn't that Marcus was indifferent to the causes but he resented being treated like street traffic in his own house. Sometimes while making dinner he would hear the back door open and Alex's boots thunk off in the hallway. Marcus would offer a how's-it-going as Alex passed by, only to be received with a grunt and, when he turned around, a stack of multicoloured photocopied squares on the kitchen table. Alex spent all his time at work or with his rats. Marcus liked animals too but there was something unwholesome about it, a flinty-eyed focus as of a saint or cult leader.

He would not serve, no, but who was he not serving? Stephen Dedalus had his Ireland, his priest-ridden dirt-poor fatherland, his own father squatting his consciousness like a golem. Marcus's background seemed flabby and permissive by comparison: Liberal middle-class parents who let him do as he pleased, a city whose watchwords were *fun* and *excess* and *live it up* and *why not*, where God was dead and everything was permitted.

The enemy as far as he could tell was so huge and remote and all-pervasive as to be insurmountable. At every turn he stocked its armoury, fed its coffers. But he would not let himself be defeated by it, not yet.

I will not serve. I will not serve. I'm not going to take it. No, I'm not going to take it, I'm not going to take it, anymore.

Then there was Flipper Week. That was when Alex, who by then had dropped out of university, decided that the cause of humanity's problems was rooted in opposable thumbs. "Think about it," he said. "Tools, civilization, slavery, capitalism, war. None of it possible without these." He wiggled them. As an experiment in what he called de-digiprivileging, Alex started taping down his thumbs with duct tape. His dexterity limited thus, his life became simplified, and he felt, he said, "free as an otter." He could still perform most tasks, albeit slowly and with some difficulty. He could walk, type, hold a beer bottle two-handed, eat. He couldn't ride a bike, use a can opener, brush his teeth, or answer the phone. What did it matter? He was de-volving and it felt right. A week turned into two and the edges of the duct tape started to fray. His hands became glued over with sweat, grime, and hair. Alex took to gnawing the tape absentmindedly, like one of his rats. Sometimes he would sit staring into space, one flipper in his mouth and the other in his lap, where one or the other of the rats worked it over, making little clacking sounds with its long amber teeth. The sight made Marcus shudder.

If things went as planned he would go straight into a post-graduate program and from there a professorship; before long he would be tenured and could immerse himself entirely in theory. He had thought his life plan was something Alex would admire—maybe it would even inspire him to quit his job at the call centre. But Alex had shown indifference, almost discomfort, whenever Marcus talked about his future. He wondered if Alex could be jealous. Then he pushed the thought down; it had some nasty pleasure in it, like sniffing a fart.

Alex walked down Van Horne Avenue, which ran parallel to the train tracks separating Mile End and Outremont from Parc Ex and Petite Patrie. It's a city of divides, he thought, St. Laurent marking the East-West Anglo-Franco schism, *east of St. Laurent* a phrase indicating all that is foreign and unfathomable to an émigré from Out West: Elvis-themed laundromats, seniors in tiger print pants and purple bouffants. Van Horne, or the train tracks it mirrors, splits north from south, the complicated system of fences and overpasses forming a bottleneck that slows the flow of trendseeking twentysomethings into the old-man coffee clubs of Little Italy. At one historical point the split may have worked to keep the immigrants of Montreal North—the Haitian, Pakistani, Ethiopian, Congolese, Ghanaian, Indian, Syrian, Lebanese, Iranian, Jamaican population—from crowing out the older arrivistes of Mile End, the Greek, Portuguese,

Ashkenazi Jewish, Quebecois *pur laine*. But now the barrier works the other way, as the young clamour ever north.

Named for the railway CEO who dreamed it into being, Van Horne should have been a majestic avenue of luxury hotels, café bistros and microbreweries. Other Van Horne creations, like the Banff Springs Hotel, the Windsor Arms, and the Queen E, occupy their railside territory with gloomy grandeur. But Montreal's Avenue Van Horne, opening with a cold storage warehouse where the street juts diagonally from St. Laurent, continues on a distinctly unglamorous arc. It was possible, Alex noted, to walk blocks along Van Horne without passing a single retail enterprise. It was all warehouses and abandoned-looking apartment buildings and empty lots. There were so many empty lots that you started to imagine a taxonomy of them, as if they could be ordered from a catalogue. The feral lot, waist deep with burdock, goldenrod and ragweed. The unsold lot, pincushioned with *À Vendre* signs. The shy lot, the defiant lot, the who-gives-a-fuck-anyway lot. The lot that doesn't know it's a lot. The fresh lot: until last week it held a building, and now it lies open, unnerving as a freshly dug grave. A square of sky sits uncovered, a vintage area of space that hasn't been seen since the building went up in 1936. And see, it's been perfectly preserved—you can't tell it from the rest of the sky around it.

Finally the sign for the muffler shop appeared, and Alex was back in civilization. Docteur Silencieux smiled from the billboard, something sinister in his name and his handsome, reassuring face. Alex gave him a nod and continued on to Parc.

Alex carried a small cardboard box carefully in front of him. The box's weight was satisfying for its size. It had a density and a diminutive heft.

Inside the box was Alex's rat, Hall.

At the end of August the yard had that kind of late-summer post-coital exhaustion; the plants seemed overripe and limp, verging on rot, but with enough bloom left that you remembered it. The flowers on the chestnut tree were gone and the leaves had darkened to oily green; there was a smell like campfires.

On the back porch, Marcus and Sally were drinking some of Marcus's homemade beer, tossing bottle caps over the fence into the neighbouring yard. Someone was barbecuing and it reminded Sally that all she had eaten that day was a bowl of lentil soup.

"Where's Alex?" Sally said.

"Burying his rat."

"Oh." She ran the back of her hand over her lips. "Simon or Garfunkle?"

"Yeah," said Marcus, "something like that."

"Poor little guy."

"Mmm."

On the other side of the fence a voice said "Here comes the cheese!"

Sally led a monthly workshop in something she called Aromemorial Therapy. She invited participants to bring an object with strong ties to a personal memory. Using a combination of distillation and alcohol infusion they created an "essence" of that object, which they bottled in brown glass containers. Uncapping the bottle releases an aroma which, Sally believed, accesses hidden memories and heals trauma.

Sally's room was full of these bottles, ones she'd made herself and ones left over from workshop participants who never came back for the second day. There were teddy bears, old shoes, notebooks, mittens, coffee mugs, all varieties of mundane knickknacks, made mute and nostalgic by the brown glass, like sepia-tinted photographs. She called it the archive of trauma.

As Alex walked down Champagneur toward the tracks, he saw the guy who panhandled in the neighbourhood race by, dragging his plaid granny stroller behind him. Alex noticed he'd gotten a haircut—a good one, in fact. Where does a homeless guy go to get a haircut? The guy reached the fence, lofted the stroller over, and took the chain-link easily, hopping it in a couple of fluid thrusts. He picked up the stroller from where it landed and sped over the tracks, repeating the movements on the opposite fence.

Alex set the box down and adjusted his shoulder bag, in which he carried a rusted trowel and a bag of seeds. It still got hot out those days; only at night did the wind sometimes carry that smell of cold glass and dead leaves. Alex picked up the box again, trying to ignore the shift of weight inside it.

Hall had died early that morning, while Alex was asleep. Around five a.m. exhaustion had overtaken his vigil, and Hall had used that opportunity to slip the surly bonds of earth, collapsing, as Alex saw when he woke up, half inside his food dish, his back feet poking straight up in the air. Alex had lifted him from the cage, cleaned him up, and wrapped him in a handkerchief. He set off for the burial on foot. Lynnie had offered to come with him but Alex declined her company. Marcus had said nothing.

In an alleyway Alex saw a woman in niqab, the shape of a narrow archway, playing soccer with a little boy. She lunged gracefully, blocking his arcs. Behind the pair a billboard showed a black and white photo of a man in his underwear. He lounged in a posture of tensed repose, like a jungle cat. Alex remembered another time in this alleyway, walking with Sally and talking about a guy they knew who took all his conquests on the same date, a tin-can barbecue and bottle of wine by the train tracks. Alex had lived here long enough that his memories had memories.

When Alex reached the hole in the fence behind the auto shop, he ducked through. The train tracks stretched in either direction. The sky here looked bigger somehow than other places in the city. The tracks were bushy with weeds, thistle and lamb's quarters and small doomed trees. He put the box down, took out the trowel, and started to dig.

"Every morning I wake up at three a.m. on the nose," Sally said, "even though I stopped bartending six months ago. That job reset my circadian rhythms to give me a boost of adrenalin in time for closing, when I had to throw everyone out, wash a bathtub's worth of dishes, put the chairs up, sweep the floor, lock up The Miracle and bike home. And now I can't stop waking up. I just lie there with my heart pounding, telling myself to go back to sleep."

The wind shifted, bringing with it the smell of Vietnamese food. The house was located at the crux of several local updrafts and the housemates could tell the direction of the wind by the smell it carried.

"A full night's sleep is an invention of capitalism," Marcus told her. "Before factories, before electricity, before industrialization, people would sleep in shifts called first sleep and second sleep. In between there is a period of wakefulness that belongs only to you. It was valued as a time of reflection and creativity. It's when peasant couples would talk to each other and fuck, and monks would pray, and poets would write." He had read this somewhere.

The back gate creaked open, and Alex came up the small path through the backyard. He looked tired, and there was a smear of dirt across his forehead. He carried a small shovel, and his empty satchel hung from one shoulder.

"Yo," said Marcus. "Got a beer for you."

"I gotta go inside," Alex said. "Oates—whatever."

"C'mon, sit for a minute. We haven't hung out in forever."

"Yeah," said Sally, "like for*ever*."

Alex looked toward the house, then folded himself in front of the mildewed sofa and leaned back against Sally's legs. She wrapped her arms around his neck and he sighed.

"Get 'er done?" said Marcus.

"Yeah. No big deal. It's over, at least."

"Cast a cold eye on life / on death; Horseman, pass by," Marcus said, quoting Yeats's tombstone. Alex nodded. He looked up, then reached over and grabbed onto Marcus's fingers. Marcus squeezed back, and their hands remained there, suspended, until Alex let go and picked up a beer by its neck.

Marcus told Alex about Abby, the girl he liked.

"She's in my Shakespeare class. She said her favourite part in *Hamlet* is when Hamlet says 'Woot weep?' to Claudius over Ophelia's grave. She said it makes Hamlet sound like a really upset owl."

"Cute," said Alex. "Did you touch her perfect body with your mind?" This was code for thinking about someone while you masturbate. I am so going to touch that perfect body with my mind, they had said to each other a million times.

"Gross, Alex," Marcus says, looking at Sally, then back to Alex. He wondered when the last time Alex got laid was.

They all watched as the shrimp-smelling wind took a plastic bag off the porch and whipped it over into the neighbouring yard. Alex stood up and slapped at his jeans. He picked up his half-empty beer, saluted them with it, and went inside.

"Do you think," Sally said, "that by letting our garbage pile up on the balcony like this we're just making more work for our neighbours?"

"Probably," said Marcus.

Sally nodded and began stuffing things into other things; paper into boxes, bottles into cans and cans into bags. Later, even when he could barely stand to be around her, Marcus would remember this image, the tendons in her neck and the clomp of her rubber boots and the careless and efficient way she handled herself, the wind making a fan of her hair.

Marcus turned to see Alex standing in the doorway. His head was tilted to one side.

"How—" said Marcus. Before he could finish Alex's hand came out fast as a snake, whipping a projectile straight at Marcus's head. It hit the side of his face and dropped into his lap. The impact was dull and wet, as though Alex had flung a soaked wad of cotton.

Marcus put his hand to his jaw and looked down. In his lap was Oates, dead, his eyes and mouth open, teeth bared in a last grimace. His testicles were bluish and touching the inside seam of Marcus's jeans. He had not gone gentle into that good night.

"Jesus *fuck*," Sally said, dropping the box she held in her hands. Alex pushed past her and ran down the porch steps and through the yard, skidded on patch of wet grass, then corrected and flew past the fence. He turned down the alley and kept going. Sally took a few steps toward the fence, then turned back to Marcus.

"Well that was majorly fucked," she said.

"Yeah," said Marcus, who now held the rat loosely in one hand. "Poor guy."

"Him or the rat?"

"Yeah," said Marcus.

What happened after that was mostly unremarkable. The two of them unlatched smoothly as a key leaving a lock. Marcus moved into a bachelor apartment in a different neighbourhood, one that smelled of croissants and smoked meat. Alex stayed on at the house, converting Marcus's old room into a workshop. Marcus kept up with the house for a while; there were bonfires, there were Sunday potluck dinners. And then, eventually, there weren't. In retrospect Marcus saw a kind of beauty in their separation, a graceful parting of ways, like a river forking in two. It was how things were meant to go. There may have been a quote about it somewhere, but Marcus couldn't remember what it is.

—

The loose end of the toilet paper in the bathroom is folded into a sharp triangle. Marcus gets no small amount of pleasure from this. It's not just an aesthetic thing. The triangle's point is a guarantee of safety and cleanliness, a little contract between the hotel and the client, assuring him that his will be the first hand to touch the dangling end of the roll after the excretory act. It's a reassurance, a promissory note.

Marcus loves hotels. Since tenure-track he's discovered in himself a capacity for leisure he never knew existed. He enters a state of near-hibernation in these rooms, leaving only when required by work, venturing no further than the vending machine down the hall for sustenance. Room service, even better.

Marcus unfolds the local paper. By the time he gets to World News he's aware that he's no longer paying attention to the stories. His attention has turned wholly inward, to the process of his bowel, which seems Machiavellian as any government.

He keeps seeing the same, he hopes, silverfish running the baseboards of the room. Its head turns left and right, looking for an opening. Something so small making a decision. He folds the paper, wipes, flushes.

Standing in front of the mirror, Marcus opens a container of dental floss and reels out a length. It is dry, like a bit of tendon. Not waxed. He looks at the packaging, which is clearly marked *Waxed*. He winds one end of the floss around an index finger, and the other end finds its corresponding digit. The floss goes in between the two front teeth, the pearly whites, the all-I-want-fors, putting him in mind of sticking a hand between two sofa cushions in search of lost change. A ginger rummaging, wary of the sticky, the soft, the yielding. Give us hard and smooth only, no weak spots or cave-ins of the flesh. The floss is arid and crisp; he feels as though he is playing his teeth with a violin bow. The tune: "How Much Is That Doggie in the Window." In G major. If the package is marked *Waxed* and the floss is palpably unwaxed, there is an alarming slippage between the sign and the signified. What could it mean?

After the bathroom ritual Marcus flops onto the bed, which is strewn with papers from the conference, and lights the second cigarette of the day. The second is always the best. The problem is the first, which is invariably awful. The difficulty is how to get to the second without the first.

He once asked Alex how he quit after a ten-year, pack-a-day habit. "Well," Alex said, "I stopped having cigarettes."

Marcus flips on the TV. He's in the mood for something that will relax him, his head chirping after a day of unlimited drip coffee, small talk and panels where colleagues ten years his junior presented papers whose brilliance made his own work seem rote. He runs his hands through his hair a few times, grateful that he still has all of it and that at thirty-seven he is still trim and energetic. So many of his fellow academics have become badger-like, soft-bellied creatures squinting behind their wire-rimmed glasses.

He finds a rerun of *ImmigRaces*, an old favourite at his former house. Part gladiator-style sporting event, part reality show, part helpful civic contribution, *ImmigRaces* took place on the grounds of the old closed-down Hippodrome. Illegal immigrants discovered by undercover police squads would be turned over to the producers of the Races, where they would be housed in barracks underneath the stadium and made to participate in a series of challenges. These ranged from obstacle courses involving pools of oatmeal and grease-coated rope swings to the devouring of live insects to recitations of hour-long oaths of allegiance from memory, in both official languages. The winner of each season's competition was granted citizenship for himself and his family. Second prize was a ticket home.

"This show is so formulaic," Alex once said. As though it was a bad thing. But the best stories are the formulaic ones, the ones where you know what's going to happen next but you watch anyway, to have that itch rubbed out, to pour full the empty glass in your head.

The show cuts to commercial. Marcus watches as a bumbling dad forgets his kid's birthday, accidentally beheads her stuffed teddy, and shrinks her blanky in the wash. When it looks like things are about to go completely off the cliff, he grinningly pulls a bag of cotton-candy-flavoured chips out of a grocery bag. There is a joyous reunion, with hugging and giggles and one well-aimed shining wink at the camera. Marcus stares at the TV, and then at the bag of cotton-candy-flavoured chips beside him. If he needed confirmation, this is it. He is the centre of the universe.

Marcus opens his phone. It's two hours later where Abby is so she should be just getting into bed, wearing her long blue cotton nightgown with the lace around the neck. She'll be reading something, a biography of an old film star maybe. Her face will be damp and sticky with night cream, her skin warm, except for her feet, which even in the July heat will be cool and dry to the touch.

"Hi babe," she says in his ear.

"Hey," he says, sighing more than he intends to.

"Go okay today?"

"Yeah, you know how it is. Another day, another dollar."

"Fourteen hours on snowshoes and wish you had pie?" She completes the Dillard quote for him.

"Mmm, pie," he says. "Yeah actually it was good. About a dozen people showed up, including the chair of the cultural studies department. She came and talked to me after, said she thought my work showed promise."

They talk more about his presentation, he asks after the kids, who are fine and asleep, and then Abby says she has to go, there's a segment on CBC's *Ideas* that she wants to listen to.

"'Night, love," she says.

"Don't forget about me."

"*Jamais.*"

He rolls over onto his stomach, brushing crumbs from the broadloom comforter. He opens the phone again.

When Sally answers she sounds less than thrilled to hear him.

"Have you been watching the Moving Day coverage?" she says.

"Yeah," Marcus lies. "Crazy stuff." He might not have watched this time but he knows the drill, it's regular as payday.

"So you saw Alex," she says. Marcus sits up. "When," he says, "on TV?"

"Yes, on TV."

"I must have missed that part."

"Uh-huh," says Sally. "Anyway he's in detention, me and some others are going to the solidarity demo tonight. You should come."

"I'm in Alberta," he says.

"Oh, well never mind then." As though he's told her he's at the grocery store.

"Sally," he says.

"Yeah?" Something in her voice, some tone beyond generic encouragement makes him go on.

"How's your. You know, the..."

"Multiple sclerosis?"

"Yeah, sorry."

"Slowly eating away at my nervous system," Sally says. A puff of air comes out of Marcus's nose. "No, sorry," she says, "I'm a jerk. It's fine. No new lesions. I'm not a babbling mess yet."

"No more so than usual, anyway," says Marcus, and Sally chuckles.

"Remember that time we dressed up as zombies and tried to get kicked out of the bank?" he says. "Alex was screaming 'class war,' but instead of arresting us they just laughed and said we were right?"

"Yeah," she says, distant. "That was nice."

"We should do that again sometime."

"Sure."

What was it Alex had said when Sally was diagnosed? "It's pointless to think about people as healthy or sick. There's only the sick and the not-yet-sick." "That's pretty grim," Marcus had said. "I actually find it quite freeing," said Alex. "We're all in it together." But Marcus would take solitude over that kind of company.

"Sally, how is he? I mean actually?"

"Oh you know. Fine. Depressed. Fine. Still working at the call centre. Dating a teenager."

"Really?"

"Well he's twenty-one."

"How come gays can do that and no one bats an eye," says Marcus, "but if I did it I'd get in trouble?"

"It's called patriarchy, Marcus."

"Yeah yeah yeah," he says. He sees the silverfish, or one of its relatives, circling the rim of the light fixture. "Sally," he says, "just because I'm not calling doesn't mean I'm not thinking about you."

"Okay. I gotta go."

"Yeah," he says. "Bye."

Depression has no needs, Marcus thinks. It makes no demands, requires nothing. All it wants is for you to stay in bed, staring at the light fixture in a hotel room. It is the opposite of hunger, the opposite of addiction. The more powerful it is the less it asks of you.

The phone rings. Marcus flips it open. "Hello," he says, "hello, hello." But all he hears is the sound of the inside of Sally's pocket. He listens. It sounds like the ocean.

He hadn't done anything out of the ordinary, he knew this. It was rather a kindness, a favour to an old friend. If Alex didn't understand at the time then surely he did now. And any bad feelings he harboured must be diluted by the sea of time that had passed, a sea that had carried Marcus here, to this hotel, this room, this bed. He knew that there was no such thing as wrong and right, only content and less content. And he was content. Content enough.

It hadn't taken long to find a good recipe. CO_2 could be created with baking soda and vinegar, and according to the website it was effective within twelve to twenty minutes. The subject sleeps, and after that his heart and respiratory system go dark.

Using a shoebox, some duct tape, and a long twirling gag-straw he found at the dollar store, Marcus had constructed an airtight chamber, except for the straw, which piped into a Mason jar with a hole punched in the lid. The whole works looked like it might have been created during a game of Hangman of the Absurd.

In Alex's room, Marcus saw that Oates had pushed all of his wood chips up against one side of his cage. He was crouched atop the beige heap, his disproportionately large balls pressed up against the wire. His sides pulsed minutely as he breathed. Marcus stuck a finger through the cage and touched his nose. Oates didn't move. Marcus squatted down so he was level with Oates' snouty face. He reached around and poked the rodent's bald sack with a fingernail.

"Neep," went Oates.

"Neep," went Marcus.

He opened the cage and reached in for the small white form, withdrew his hand, careful not to press too hard against the throbbing sides. In the warmth left by the rat's body he put a note, next to which he would lay poor Oates when it was over and the rats were joined again:

Cast a cold Eye
On Life, on Death.
Horseman, pass by!

But that was so long ago.

Maitland

Yes, Frieda had met Maitland before. Or she knew his name. He was one of those men who was always called by his last name, probably even as an adolescent. In some cases this is done out of respect, in others out of condescension; occasionally the name just seems to fit. His first name was something forgettable and childish, like Kevin or Matt. So he was Maitland.

His two-year-old daughter straddled his neck, playing with his tufty black hair. He was plump and squinted, his hair receding but not thinning. A decent-looking man, one who would never run the risk of ugliness or beauty with some strong, striking facial feature. He would pass gently into middle and old age, Frieda thought, his round, somewhat sly face a reassurance to his wife and friends, who would always see the Maitland they knew in it.

He had spoken directly to Frieda only once during the Seder, to make a comparison between the *afikoman*, which is split in two, and the holy trinity, which is split in three but still indivisible.

"See, what my family did," Frieda said, "our tradition was for the *kids* to hide the matzah and the *parents* to look for it." This as Maitland's son Maurice was being coached to find the hidden afikoman with cries of "warm... warmer... warmer... cold! Freezing cold!"

"And every year we'd spend ages finding the perfect hiding spot. Once we wrapped it in a sandwich baggie and put it in the toilet tank. I can't remember where else," Frieda said. "Anyway, every year the same thing happened, which was that when it came time for them to look for the afikoman, our parents would just pay us off to go find it for them." A round of clapping and cheers went up as Maurice tentatively grasped the edge of the cloth that held the afikoman, which was poking out from under a sofa cushion.

"I just thought it was funny," Frieda said, "that every year we acted like this time really for real the parents were going to look for it, even though we had absolutely no evidence they would."

"Such is the nature of belief," Rachel said.

"Right," said Frieda, "though I think we just liked to imagine them looking for it."

Maitland was the best friend of Rachel's husband, Laurent. Frieda and Rachel had been friends in university, and Frieda still thought well of Rachel but they had drifted, as university friends do. Once or twice a year they saw each other at some social event: a wedding, a weekend at Laurent's family cabin in St. Adele, a Passover Seder or Hanukkah party. Laurent was a friendly bear of a man, seemingly destined to be a patriarch, but thus far he and Rachel had not produced.

"We've been trying," Rachel confided to Frieda, "but so far nothing's taken." Frieda wondered to herself what "trying" meant. It meant having sex, right? There was a time when she would have said this to Rachel, but now she just nodded.

Instead it was Maitland and his wife, Sylvie, who showed up at each gathering with multiplying evidence of their fertility. Sylvie was currently pregnant with her third; her body seemed completely given over to reproduction. She was cushiony and comfortable to look at. A Québecoise Madonna, Frieda thought. Hips wide and soft, breast ample, an organic habitat for the young. Tiny baggies of Cheerios and crackers appeared from her pockets like so many loaves and fishes and her fingers dangled toys, pacifiers.

Frieda herself had once become pregnant, quite without trying. When she told the guy, he seemed unconvinced. "How do you know?" he said.

"A woman knows," Frieda replied.

"Really?"

"No, I peed on the stick."

"Oh."

At a karaoke bar Frieda sang Loretta Lynn's "One's On the Way," trying to be funny; the guy choked on a swig of beer and had to be pounded on the back by the bartender. He stuck around long enough to drive her home from the clinic, then moved to Calgary. Frieda thought he had maybe gone into the oil biz.

On Frieda's left was Sophie, a coworker of Rachel's. Sophie leaned over the gefilte fish and took a sniff, then turned down the corners of her mouth. "*Mais, c'est quoi ça?*" she said.

"Pickled fish," Frieda said. She heaped hot pink, toxic-looking horseradish on her own slice, then quartered it.

"I don't understand how you can eat that."

"It's kind of an acquired taste," Rachel said.

"Not for me," said Frieda, mouth full. "I was born with a piece of schmaltz herring in my mouth." There was a rim of pink-tinted brine on her plate.

Sophie shook her head. "*Dégueulasse*," she said. She was a pretty, delicate-faced girl in an asymetrical shirt, the kind you found at a boutique stocked with local designers who use a lot of gingham and paisley. She would be the target audience for these boutiques, Frieda thought—middle-class quirky, retro without the mildew and pit-stains. Nostalgic for the accoutrements of pre–Quiet Revolution days. A lover of ornamental buttons.

Frieda herself was wearing a hot, itchy wool dress that had been her mother's. As a teenager she had defiled it, cutting off the cowl-neck with pinking shears and stitching a sloppy neckline into the weave. The sleeves were long and flared at the wrists. She thought it made her look vaguely nunnish, in a way that positively accented her somewhat severe Russian features.

She took another look at Maitland. He was telling a story about how a park by his and Sylvie's house was closed to visitors because someone had been illicitly tapping the maple trees. "But is it homeless squeegee kids or neighbourhood yuppie locavores? No one knows."

"He's joking," Sophie said. "Are you joking?"

What no one there knew was that Frieda had known Maitland years ago, if only by name. When she was nineteen Frieda had a best friend, a brilliant, ascerbic girl named Dori. Dori had met Maitland in a human anatomy class she was taking as an advanced undergrad and they became friends. Through Dori Frieda heard about this guy, this older med student with a funny name. He was a joker, charming, possibly less smart than Dori but a dedicated worker and problem solver. She admired him, that was clear; she said he had a bright future.

One night at a party Dori got drunk and fell asleep in

the host's bedroom. She woke up to find Maitland's hand under her dress, inside her leggings. There was some confusion, and then they rejoined the party. All this Dori told to Frieda the next morning. She was calm, in a way that Frieda had learned to be wary of.

A week later a letter came for Dori. A typewritten false apology: *The temptation... your beauty... my inebriated state. I hope you won't...* Signed, *Maitland*.

Dori's response was scathing. She systematically demolished each sentence of his letter, ending with the sentiment that the idea of him becoming a doctor made her sick to her stomach. *Never talk to me again,* she concluded. *Go to hell. Dori.* She deposited the letter in the school's internal mail system, dry-eyed. Then she wept, bitterly, for hours, while Frieda rubbed her back in slow circles and tried to be soothing.

"What an ass. He's the one that looks bad, not you."

"No one's ever called me beautiful before," Dori said between sobs.

Two weeks later Dori wasn't sleeping. She was acting erratic—dancing at after-hours clubs till 7:00 a.m., eating nothing but cereal. Plucking her eyebrows completely out so she looked like a gaunt baby. Frieda suggested she go to the university. "You have to tell someone," she said. "He should be expelled. Or, hey, I know. We can make posters of his face that say WANTED FOR RAPE and put them up around campus. Really, you know, make his life shitty."

But Dori refused. "I was drunk," she said. "You think anyone's going to say I wasn't asking for it?" She stayed quiet, avoided Maitland. By the end of the semester she was back to her usual self, and finished the year with top marks, as everyone knew she would.

What Frieda couldn't figure out was what Maitland was doing in her life now, and what she was meant to do about it. Dori—Dori was probably over it. A psychiatrist at a free downtown clinic, she counselled abused women, homeless teens, people with traumas like open wounds. She had other things to worry about. When Frieda saw her she seemed taut, focused, her laugh a spray of gunfire. But Frieda hardly saw her.

She watched Maitland. He seemed a man at peace with himself, padded by the accoutrements of domestic life. Family man, provider, surgeon, drinker of cocktails, lover of Al Green. She had the impression not of a brittle shell of armour but of thick durable layers of hide that she could never hope to pierce. A whale-man, blubbered over, happily sucking krill. How happily, she didn't know.

Sylvie hoisted her daughter onto her lap and began to croon to her. This lap, though wide, was running out of surface area as her belly pushed out; soon Christine would have to straddle her hip. The sadness of the middle child. Sylvie thought of her own sisters, Maude and Catherine. Maude, the eldest, aloof and precocious. And coddled Catherine, Princess Katerina, whose ears and toes the whole family exclaimed over: So pink! So plump! So perfect! "Soon you will be a big sister," she whispered to Christine, "and that means you have a very important job to do. You must learn to adore, because it is through adoration that we reach our highest selves."

Christine yawned and touched her ears. This was a habit she'd developed lately, when she was tired or nervous— placing cupped hands over her ears like a monkey that hears no evil.

The first time Maurice took the school bus home he cried because of the noise. "It hurts my ears. I don't want to do that anymore."

Sylvie was sympathetic but unyielding and now Maurice rode the bus with striped earmuffs on, whatever the weather. Maitland told him they were made out of a magic substance that would not only shield his eardrums from pain but could allow him to hear people's thoughts. "But only nice thoughts," Sylvie said. "Nothing scary or mean."

Christine's eyes were drooping and Sylvie wondered when they would leave. Laurent had his guitar out and he and Maitland were trying to set the Jewish prayers to a Bob Marley tune. The heavy, oily food sat in her gut, pressed against her womb. Everything was a variation on beige: the chicken, the casserole, the fish, the baked carrots, the symbolic flatbread smeared with apple-nut paste. The Festival of Beige, it should be called. Tomorrow she would make Maitland and the children something light and colourful, a salad with pear and blueberry and mango, a slice of ham blushing like a newlywed.

She felt Christine go heavy as she dropped into sleep, while at the same time the creature in her womb stirred. They were on opposite schedules, the fetus waking only when the older two were settled down, like it knew something. Sylvie felt languidly aroused. Pregnancy made her at home in her body in a way she had never experienced before, made her crave Maitland's attention like she had only felt previously in the early days of their courtship. He was like a child himself, her Maitland, his short bouncy cock like a toy he wanted her to appreciate. When he pressed himself into the flesh of her rear (both of them on their sides, since her growing belly made any other iteration uncomfortable) and she adjusted her hips so he could enter her, she felt a pure and uncomplicated joy entirely untainted by lust. "This is fun," he'd say. "I like you." "I like you too," she would say. Sylvie checked her watch again. Perhaps if they left within the hour they would have ten minutes to spare before Maitland fell asleep.

Rachel looked thin, Sylvie thought. Her head seemed huge on her neck, a cartoon head, or a toddler's. She did not have that dry, brittle look that childless women get at a certain age, but if she didn't hurry up it would catch her. She was thin-skinned, prone to crow's feet. You worried about a person like Rachel, a genuinely kind girl who people took advantage of. Like Frieda. Her oval face and kinky hair, parted in the centre and pulled back in a barrette. A perpetually dissatisfied girl, a whiner, a loud-mouth. You never felt at home around her, but if you left her out you'd never hear the end of it. Sylvie had tried to engage her in conversation earlier but Frieda had only cackled and waved her hand, saying something that was both self-effacing and condescending. Sylvie watched her stuff a piece of buttered cracker in her mouth, crumbs catching on her black dress.

Sylvie thought that she would never wish for the power of Maurice's earmuffs, never in a thousand years.

They had bumped into each other in the hallway outside the bathroom, Sylvie emerging and Frieda going in.

"What are your stories about?" Sylvie had asked, sensing Frieda's awkwardness. She had heard something of these stories from Rachel, that Frieda wrote them, even published them sometimes.

"Oh," Frieda had laughed, snorted almost. "Nothing."

"They must be about something."

Frieda made a serious face and folded her fingers. "The unspeakable futility of the search for ethics in an unethical world." Then she laughed again. Sylvie laughed too, in sympathy rather than amusement.

They got to the Ten Plagues.

"This is my favourite part," Frieda whispered to no one in particular.

"Daddy, what means pestilence?" Maurice said.

"Boils," said Maitland. "Remember when you had the chicken pox?"

"Ick," said Sophie.

"No," Frieda said. "Boils is boils. Pestilence is something different."

"Either way," Maitland said, "Bad news for the Egyptians!"

They counted ten drops from their wine glasses, dotting their napkins or plates, while Frieda and Rachel recited in blundering Hebrew. When they got to death of the firstborn Frieda couldn't help glancing at Maitland, to see if he was affected by the callousness of the Hebrew god. He made waggly fingers at Maurice. "Watch out! The God of Israel's gonna getcha!" His hands were hairy and vital, like well-fed animals. Maurice squealed and ducked under the table.

"This reminds me of something," Frieda said, indicating her wine-spotted napkin, "but at the moment I can't seem to think of what." She looked at Sylvie, who was holding her open-mouthed toddler on her lap with one hand and resting the other on the back of Maitland's chair. Her glasses caught the light in such a way that she seemed to have no eyes. Eyeless in Gaza, Frieda thought. That was from what? *Samson Agonistes.* The brutal strongman with only two weaknesses: his hair, and his love of women. She bit down on a piece of celery and looked again at Sylvie.

The children were asleep. All the wine and most of the food was gone, and the guests were trudging through the last few songs and prayers.

"I just think it's ironic," said another guest, a girl called Sharon, "how the Jews were once oppressed, and now they're the oppressors."

"Isn't it, though?" said Frieda, and took a large gulp from her glass. "So *very* ironic. Thank you for pointing that out."

"Time will make monkeys of us all," said Maitland.

"Fools, cheri," said Sylvie. "Time will make *fools* of us all."

"Please," said Laurent, "Let's not talk politics at the table."

"Where else should we talk about them?" said Sharon.

"I agree," said Frieda. "'Tis the season!" She felt a bit much right then, flushed and giddy, and was ready to get into it.

"I mean," said Sharon, "here we are enjoying Rachel's delicious dinner, and meanwhile on the Left Bank children are starving because of Israeli occupation." Rachel nodded, her chin trembling.

"It's a shame," Sophie said.

"The Left Bank?" said Frieda.

"Look, I spilled my ten drops," Laurent said, "and I think we all understand that our joy always comes at the cost of someone else's sorrow. Right?"

"Hear hear," said Maitland.

"So let's just put all that aside for a bit, shall we? We're not going to fix the world's problems tonight, so we may as well try to enjoy each other's company." He put his arm around Rachel, who was now openly crying. She held her spotted napkin to her face and her shoulders heaved.

"It's okay, honey," Sophie said. "Don't cry. It's okay."

"B'seder," Frieda said.

"What?" said Sylvie.

"B'seder—it means 'it's okay.' The literal meaning is 'in order,' which is why this is called a seder—because we do it in order. But colloquially it means 'fine, good, a-okay.'"

"So this would be a b'seder seder?" Maitland said. Rachel laughed, not a real laugh but the kind of laugh that signalled she was ready to stop crying.

"I'm okay," she said. "Really. B'seder." Laurent picked up an empty wine bottle, peering at the bottom optimistically. He overturned it, and a trickle of red dampened the tablecloth. "Whoopsie," he said.

"What now?" said Maitland.

"Well," said Frieda, "since Passover is about telling stories, and revisiting the past, I have a story I'd like to tell." She felt the twin weights of Sylvie's pale eyes on her.

"Go on," said Sharon.

"It's about a woman," Frieda said.

"I like it already," said Maitland.

There was no traffic on the drive back to NDG. The kids were sleeping like proverbial angels, Christine in her car seat and Maurice buckled in beside her. Maitland was driving. On four glasses of wine he was still a better driver than Sylvie, who didn't trust her instincts sober. Sylvie's sensual mood had passed and she was achy, feet swollen. Maitland was quiet, a hand on the wheel and the other on her knee.

"You're quiet," she said.

He yawned. "Just sleepy, babe."

Through the windshield she watched the lights of the city

appear as they ascended the mountain.

"I never get tired of this view," she said. "Sometimes I think I'm bored of this city, I'm ready for something new, but then I see a sight like this, and I fall in love all over again."

Maitland smiled in front of him and made a murmur of agreement. The car dipped and rose.

"That was quite a story," Sylvie said.

"The Passover story? Yes, it's very interesting," Maitland said.

"Yes. But the other story. The one that Rachel's friend told. Frieda."

Maitland was silent. He took his hand from her leg and placed it on the wheel. Then he said, very quietly, "She's quite the little bitch."

Sylvie let her breath out slowly. She hadn't noticed she was holding it. "I just don't see how it was relevant," Sylvie said. Maitland looked at her askance for a moment, then turned his eyes back to the curving road. "Why would she tell a story like that? To make herself feel better? To right a wrong? What difference does it make, now? Things that happened in the past should stay there. I don't see how it's relevant," she repeated.

"Sometimes, Sylvie, you only see what you want to see." His voice was not bitter but she sensed bitterness from somewhere within him. A bitter smell, like cherry pits.

Sylvie tightened her scarf around her shoulders. "Is that it? I suppose that could be it. I don't know." They passed the lookout point and the road began to descend. Sylvie kept talking. She couldn't seem to stop. She needed to talk it out. "I don't know what I'm saying. The choices people make. I'm not sure I understand myself. What good does it do, to talk about the wrongs of the past? To make ourselves relive them over and over. We only fuel our anger that way. You don't fight fire with fire. You fight fire with *water.*"

"If you're going to hit me," Maitland said, "can I at least pull over first?"

Sylvie began to cry. She cried quietly, so as not to wake the children.

"You want me to be angry at you," she said finally, "but I refuse. I am not that kind of person."

"Okay," Maitland said.

They went on in silence. Sylvie tried to feel sadness or sympathy for that girl so many years ago, the one betrayed by a friend who liked her too much, but found she could muster only a detached pity.

"What's the point?" she said again.

A pair of yellow eyes appeared fifty feet in front of the windshield. Sylvie heard Maurice say a single word, *Papa*, and then Maitland was swerving into the oncoming lane. There was a clattering sound that seemed to be coming from inside Sylvie's body but was not, and her fetus flipped a full one hundred and eighty degrees and arched its body like a fish. The tires skidded on the moist pavement and then the anti-lock mechanism clicked in, the car swung out and around, and suddenly they were motionless on the outside shoulder, facing the wrong direction. Sylvie did and did not want to turn around. She did, slowly. Christine was still asleep in her carrier, her bangs stuck to her hot forehead. Sylvie touched her cheek, and she fluttered her lids and sighed. Maurice was wide-eyed. "What was it?"

"It was a deer," Sylvie said.

"There are no deer in this park," Maitland said. "It must have been a dog."

"A big dog," Maurice said. "Maybe it was a werewolf."

"Maybe," Maitland said.

"Did we hit it?"

"No," said Maitland. "*Câlisse*, that was close." His hands were shaking. He rested them on the steering wheel and bent his head forward onto his wrists.

"It was a deer," Sylvie said.

Helga Volga

When Abby and Marcus walk home they do this thing where they pretend they've just met and are going home together for the first time.

"This your place?" Abby says.

"Yup," says Marcus.

"Nice."

"Thanks," says Marcus. "I try to keep up."

It's not as funny as it used to be, but Abby thinks they're both afraid of what will happen if they stop.

I can't talk about it right now, Marcus said.

They live together but they're not married and never will be, because they don't believe in things like obligation. At least Marcus doesn't, and Abby is more or less indifferent. It didn't seem to matter when they first met, because when they got together it was with the sense of being superior creatures who didn't need rules. They attended friends' weddings with mildly amused condescension. They ate their cake and drank their mojitos and toasted themselves and their ungovernable love. But last June Abby watched her childhood best friend walk down the aisle and thought, there's something sexy about a contract.

And then this morning, he calls her from work.

I have to tell you something bad, but I can't talk about it right now.

There is no response to this, or at least none that will not lead to an argument. Isn't it funny how you can find yourself saying words that if you heard them on a TV sitcom you would turn to your partner and go "Oh please, that's not how real people talk."

So Abby said, "Yes honey, of course, we'll talk later."

She puts Stacey in the highchair and tries to feed her a grilled cheese while Stacey makes noises like a pterodactyl. These days everyone's giving their baby girls old-fashioned names: Olive, Maude, Mabel, Gladys, names Abby remembers from visiting her mother on the Alzheimer's ward. But she loves her girls' clean names, names without a past.

She has given Angela a hollowed-out egg to paint with her watercolours. Earlier she poked a hole in the top and bottom of the egg with a sewing needle and carefully blew the yolk out. The shell is so light and delicate it makes her fingers ache to touch it.

Now Angela considers the egg, turning it over and over. She lays it gently on her placemat and crushes it with her small fist.

"Oh sweetie," Abby says, "why did you do that?"

Angela looks up at her, puzzled. "I wanted to see all of it at once," she says.

After lunch it's nap time. Angela gets a blue foam mat and a blankie, and Stacey goes in the white wooden crib, which used to be Abby's. Angela has a case of the wiggles so Abby has to lie down and hook a leg over her to get her to fall asleep.

Who is it, she wonders. One of his co-workers? The girl from the party? Helga Volga? Of course, it's always Helga Volga. As she watches Angela sleeping, a tiny bubble of spit escaping her lips, Abby gets an intense ache in her forearms. She has to rub them together like a cricket, and when that doesn't work she squeezes them between her knees.

When they were a new couple, Abby and Marcus invented a fictitious woman so they could talk about the possible directions their relationship could take. It was easier, somehow, to have a concrete focus rather than an abstract, hovering cloud of uncertainty.

It started when Marcus was planning to travel Europe for a few months. Abby was caring for her mother and couldn't leave, and in any case felt too old to hoist a backpack and share sleeping quarters with a dozen snoring Australians.

"I want you to have your freedom," she told Marcus. "Part of travelling is, you know, experimentation."

This word made Marcus feel like he was going to work on the Manhattan Project. "I don't want to experiment, I love you," he said.

"One has nothing to do with the other," she said. "You'll meet a beautiful woman named Helga Volga or something, and she'll be like 'Come back to my castle in the Caucasus, handsome foreigner,' and I don't want you to start thinking of me as like the old ball and chain."

Marcus started to protest but Abby kept talking. "Just make sure you're careful, because Helga has chlamydia and I don't want you bringing it back here and giving it to me."

"Okay, but really, it's not going to happen."

"And she's not allowed to come and live here either."

"Right. Um... can we keep in touch through letters?"

"Yes, but no phone calls," Abby said, smiling.

After that, Helga Volga became a stand-in for anyone in their relationship that wasn't them. At parties they would select people for each other and designate them Helga Volga, the most likely candidate for an affair. When they found themselves trapped in a tired and spiralling conversation about their relationship, one or another would sigh and say "If only Helga Volga were here. She would know what to do." After one such exchange, Abby took a piece of pink chalk and wrote WWHVD? on the wall above the doorway. Eventually all they had to do was point to the writing and their argument would seem funny and absurd in light of their love and generosity toward each other.

"Will Helga Volga be there?" Abby would sometimes ask when Marcus announced that he was going to a party at a friend's studio, or to a show in a warehouse loft, or for drinks at The Miracle. If he said no, there was a possibility that Abby would join him, though often as not she'd stay home, listening to records and reading, or sketching in her notebook, or just sitting in her armchair, smoking, with John or Alice Coltrane on the turntable.

At the beginning Marcus only ever said no. And he never thought to ask her the question. One evening Abby picked up her shoulder bag and told him she was going to an art opening at a studio in the East End.

"But you hate vernissages," Marcus said.

"It's an old friend," she said, and Marcus pictured one of Abby's art school companions, a feather-haired girl in a Laura Ashley dress, or the one with the multicoloured dreadlocks. Marcus had always felt like this girl may have wanted to sleep with him, but her show of public and exuberant lesbianism kept getting in the way.

"Are you going right now?" he said. "I can be ready in ten."

"Well, I don't know," Abby said. "Helga Volga might be there."

"Oh." Marcus instantly revised the image of the old friend. A gangly tattooed boy with a thatch of mink-black hair. A sculptor with strong calloused hands. Someone in a band.

"Oh, well, okay, then have a good time, I guess."

"Thanks!" Abby seemed not to pick up on the anxiety in his voice, taking his wishes at their best. Which is how he meant them, he really did.

When the door had closed, Marcus stood in front of the record shelf for a long time. Finally he pulled out Leonard Cohen's *Songs from a Room*. He put it on.

After that, *yes* became a possibility. And from a possibility, a certainty.

The cat, who was once very fat, is now very thin, so when she sits on her haunches her flesh hangs down over her feet, as though she's wearing a ball gown. When she's hungry she hovers by Abby's legs and makes a series of high-toned upbeat enquiries. These Abby answers by getting up off the floor where she's been lying next to Angela and going to the kitchen, while the cat trots along, almost tripping Abby in her excitement. Sometimes when the cat's cries become too much for her, Abby will shut her in the bathroom, where the cool tile and plant life calms her. Once Abby retrieved the cat to find she had defecated in the bathtub, directly into the drain, like target practice.

Abby's learned to tell when Marcus is setting out on a crush. It starts with a discussion of some random information, some factoid that Marcus would otherwise find silly or irrelevant.

"Have you heard of synesthesia?"

"Yeah," Abby will say.

"It's this condition where your senses are crossed and you can, like, hear colours and see smells."

"I know. There was a special about it on the CBC. We listened to it together."

"Alice has synesthesia."

"Really."

"Yeah."

"How do you know?"

"She told me that when she hears 'Wednesday', she sees green."

"That doesn't count."

"She said she thinks of lemonade as pointy."

"If that counted then everyone in the world has synesthesia."

"I find it super interesting," he'll say.

The next thing he'll find super interesting will be her eyes, and her opinions on contemporary music and art, and her legs, and eventually her bed. And for a little while Abby will have nights to herself, to sketch and read and sit in her armchair, listening.

"Who do you think knows more about women," she asked Marcus once, "someone who's dated a lot of them or someone who is one?" It was a serious question. But now she sees that knowledge comes neither from first-hand experience nor rigorous study. Both of these things make knowledge more likely, the way going out into a storm makes getting hit by lightning more likely than staying home and watching TV. But neither guarantees it.

Abby's hair aches. She reaches up and pulls her ponytail out of its elastic, massaging her scalp with her hands. It's so easy, she thinks. It's so easy to tell ourselves that what we do is normal, that there is order and logic to everything. She thinks about her friend Liz, in the time between when Liz had a nervous breakdown and when she got better. She told Abby "I would lie on the floor of my parents' house and think, My God, we live on a *planet*."

Marcus calls to say he's picking up Thai on his way home so don't bother with dinner. Then he says, "I can't wait to see you."

"Okay," Abby says. When she hangs up her hands are shaking. Her face hurts, and she realizes she's been grinding her teeth to the rhythm of a song in her head. From the kitchen come what sound like the cries of the loneliest, most despondent cat in the universe. "I fed you," Abby says, "what else can there be?" She goes into the bathroom and closes the door.

Their governing philosophy was one of abundance. They knew that love was a resource whose volume increased as it was used, like bottomless coffee at a diner—the more you drink, the more refills you get. Or like a muscle that needs to be worked in order to grow. But now Abby wonders if perhaps they were wrong to be so generous with their feelings. Maybe a better approach is one of scarcity. She finds herself wanting to hoard.

It's not that she's worried Marcus will leave her—he's old-fashioned when it comes to the daughters, and generally averse to change. She's not even really bothered by the idea of him with another woman, or only superficially bothered. What disgusts her most is the thrill of gratification she feels when she knows for certain about Helga Volga.

At a party once she watched Marcus dance with a woman she vaguely knew. It was dark, the air blue and heavy with cigarette smoke. The woman reached over and took his beer by the neck. She sipped it, and as she handed it to him she kissed him on the mouth. He kissed her back. When they separated he looked up and saw her, Abby, watching. He looked at her over the woman's head. He smiled as if to say, what's a guy like me doing here? And Abby felt a stab of gruesome pleasure, like worrying a loose tooth with your tongue. Pleasure that she was losing, that Marcus was more popular, more attractive than she was, that he was getting what he wanted, something she could never achieve. A sweet self-pitying surrender, like the actor's graceful fall onto the sword. It was the only way she could get it.

Abby pulls up her leggings. The toilet, as always, says "shadow" as she flushes it. She wonders if it says this to everyone, or just her. In Brazil, does the toilet speak Portuguese? Or does it still say "shadow," keeping its meaning to itself.

The kids are starting to wake up. Stacey always sighs loudly and continuously just before she comes to, like she's reluctant to leave the dreamworld. Abby lifts her out of the crib and lays her over a shoulder. She carries her into the kitchen, where she notices she's filled the cat's bowl with blueberries.

The phone rings again.

"Four times," says Abby's sister Lydia. "Can you believe it?"

"Wow," says Abby. Lydia and her childhood sweetheart husband divorced amicably a year ago, and since then Lydia has been embarking on a journey of sexual discovery. She likes to tell Abby about how many orgasms she has, reporting dutifully to her after each session.

"Yeah, well, I'm sure it's nothing compared to what you're used to."

"Everyone is different," says Abby.

"See you Friday," says Lydia.

94

Once, while dropping Angela off at preschool, she overheard another mother say to her son, "well honey, it's hard for parents to invite *all* the kids in the class to a party."

It's well after eight when Marcus gets in. The kids are sleeping. They eat the Thai and watch a couple episodes of *Other People's Lives*. Then they lie in bed and do things that would be preludes to sex if they hadn't been together so long.

Marcus insists on trimming his pubic hair down to a lawn-like covering. The tree looks bigger when you cut back the foliage, he says. But is that really true? Doesn't the foliage contribute to an all-over sense of abundance?

Marcus is a selfish lover, but due to some fluke his selfishness overlaps with Abby's own: what he wants to do is, miraculously, exactly what she wants him to do. In that regard they are matched like cup and saucer.

Afterwards he says "Lie on me," so she does, chest to chest like a PB & J sandwich, sticky side in. Her face presses into the mattress beside his neck. Gradually he begins to snuffle. Without looking at him she cups the side of his face with her hand and strokes his stubble, from the earlobe down to the neck.

"Whatever it is, we'll get through it," she says. She rolls off and looks at him. His eyes are spilling over kind of messily. He doesn't cry in drops but with an all-over seepage, as if the water table in him is rising.

He sighs shakily then, and takes Abby's hand.

"Remember my old friend Sally?"

She nods. Oh yes. Simultaneous to the memory of this friend is the remembrance of the fact that cicadas can live underground for up to seventeen years.

Marcus swallows, then takes a breath. "She had a, what...

A brain scan, I guess. And it came back irregular, and I guess it's MS. The doctors say."

"Multiple sclerosis?" Abby says. He just looks at her. Then he moans and covers his face.

"Oh sweetie," Abby says, "oh babe." She is surprised at how normal he looks when he cries. Abby tries to cover his body with hers, and thinks Thank God, thank God, thank God. That that's all it is. Thank God.

Frenching the Eagle

We close our eyes. It is important that our eyes stay closed for the duration of the talk, because this is about finding a special space, and our special space is not outside our faces. So we keep them closed until the facilitator says we can open them. The facilitator is me. Now we put our minds in our bellies. What does that mean? It means be present in the centre of your body, because that is where the breath begins. In our bellies. We put our mind there. What do we see? Not a lot. That's right. That's because we're not practiced. We are amateurs at belly vision, and we don't know how to see from the inside. But we don't worry. We are here to learn.

We relax every muscle in our bodies. We see each muscle as a shape made out of jelly, a moulded pudding pop, and we allow it to dissolve into the sea of consciousness. We breathe. We become aware of how our bodies are in contact with the floor, all the aches and pains we hold in our muscles, and then we let them go. We see our aches and pains as butterflies that we are releasing into the sky. They flutter upwards, and some are eaten by birds. We let them go. We understand our conscious mind as a sheet flapping on a laundry line, somewhere far in the distance. We let it flap.

Now we picture an object for each colour of the rainbow.

For instance, red might be an apple, a sunset, a spot of blood.

What might orange be? Yes, an orange, that's good. Or maybe an orange ball, or an orange cup. Yes, or a sunset.

Yellow: a banana, ripe. Yes, or a sunset.

Green: a banana, unripe. Yes, or for red we could see one of those red bananas from Panama, but let's stick with green. A blade of grass, a forest in the unfurling of summer.

Blue: the sea, in which our muscle-shapes have dissolved. The sky, in which our aches and pains have fluttered away.

And last is violet. What do we see for violet? A flower, or a silken violet robe. A velvet cushion with deep and lustrous pile.

Now we see ourselves in a hallway. We don't name the hallway, but we see it. Once we can see a place without using words, we will be able to leave our bodies behind. We walk down the hallway, over the carpet, passing many doors on our right and our left. Which door will we choose? We choose a door. We place a hand on the knob and open the door. We go through the door.

In front of us we see a large marble staircase leading down. There are twenty-one steps. When we have stepped off the last step, we will be in our special place. We count together.

Twenty-one.

Twenty.

Nineteen.

Eighteen.

Seventeen.

Sixteen.

Fifteen.

Fourteen.
Thirteen.
Twelve.
Eleven.
Ten.
Nine.
Eight.
Seven.
Six.
Five.
Four.
Three.
Two.
We are ready to enter our special place.
One.
Now, we put on our high heels.

We put on our high heels because we are becoming something else, and to become something else we need to change the way we stand. Here is some pertinent information: personality begins at the sole. We understand this on the level of the animal within us, but our human bodies forget. It is an interesting fact that in French, the heels are called "*les talons.*" Talons. Does that make us think of anything? The French understand the relationship between the animal self and the human body. That is why they are the most sensual people. Why do you think they call it "frenching?" The eagle is a bird with chronic halitosis, because it eats mainly raw meat. Not many veggies on the mountain cold and craggy. But we are not here to judge or comment. We are here to be. We are here to embrace the eagle, to french it. Until we become it.

Becoming. It's a beautiful word, isn't it? It's what we say of a girl who is turned out just right, just the cat's pyjamas: Isn't she becoming? Soon, that's what they will say about you.

Good.

We notice how the shoes change the organization of our bodies. How many of us suffer under the impression that our bodies are imperfect communication devices, that they speak to us in a language we do not understand? We observe the increased arch in the back, the way the hips and breasts form a balance on either end, like dumbbells. It doesn't matter what we're wearing. Any outfit will do. Even in a baggy jumpsuit we can assume a certain degree of physical intelligibility, just by paying heed to how we stand. Even if we were in a straightjacket, even if we were swathed in canvas like a boat, our arms all twisted behind us, we would say, Okay, how can I turn this situation to my advantage? The answer is: elegance. Elegance is our sorcerer's wand.

The heels are not elegance. The heels are the container for elegance. The rest is us.

All of us have done things that make us unable or unfit to walk amongst the majority of people. Some of us are thieves. Some of us—many of us—are whores. Some of us are murderers, child-killers, father-killers, lover-killers, husband-killers. Man-eaters. That is a joke, though most of us have tasted man-flesh in one form or another. Some of us did it out of necessity. Some of us did it out of sadness, or loneliness, or temporary insanity. Some of us did it because the voices wouldn't stop. Some of us were too poor to be able to buy food for our baby, so we went out one night and shot a bank manager, just because. Because that's what happens when you interfere with the natural order of womanhood. We are not talking about hunt and gather here, tend and nurture. We are talking about the mountain cold and craggy. We are talking about frenching the eagle. We are talking about a woman's natural predisposition toward preservation of the integrity and beauty of the self. Another word for this is: elegance. Do you see where we're headed here?

Our crimes are pitiful. But they are not us. We must remember to separate the crime, which is a product of the human body and its reachings and failings, from the animal self, which is us. When we feel fear, we repeat our mantra:

We are safe. We are loved. We are precious and above all elegant.

Our mantra, if said correctly, can reverse the order of things. It is like an earthquake that happens backwards. Vases fly up onto tables and heal themselves, two broken slabs become a bridge, children emerge from piles of rubble. Our mantra is our defence against everything that threatens to undo us, to uglify us, to make us into cattle. Have you ever seen a cow you could describe as elegant? Exactly. We repeat our mantra, as needed.

Don't be afraid if it doesn't come right away. Elegance is not easy. It is about staying loose while maintaining the strictest discipline, holding tight while letting go. Like so many things. We know a person, a man, who once fell two storeys off a roof and came away with no more than bruises because he had enough presence of mind to go completely limp as he fell. It sounds easy, but you try it—relinquishing control as the ground rushes up and the wind hoots past your ears. It is the opposite of easy.

Here is a useful tip. Many of us are haunted people. If we see a ghost, if we are afraid of ghosts, we must eat a piece of meat in front of him. Raw meat? It doesn't matter. Any kind of meat. A chicken leg. Why is this? Because ghosts don't like to be reminded of the world of flesh. And to eat meat is to show a ghost that you are a master of the world of flesh. After that, he will show you some respect.

How did we get here, to this point of pain and antagonism, to these jumpsuits which are orange, orange like a cup or a ball or a sunset. To these smallish rooms, each smaller than the last, to the bus that takes us not like a lover but like a heart attack. From the bus we watch Harvey's roll past us and Wendy's and Timmy Ho's, all the familiar names of our childhood, now gathered here to say goodbye to us on our final journey, though it is possible they have been saying goodbye to us all along because the more we think about it the more we realize we have always been on this bus. From when we were crapped ungloriously out into the world until now, and we will stay here evermore. It is a kind of death, this bus.

We must calm ourselves. We are in our special space. We are safe. We are loved. We are precious and above all elegant.

The bus rolls on. Out the window we can now see the white marble stone of the courthouse, the house of court, of courting, of courtship, which is another word for dating, a coincidence that strikes us now as funny, since we only have one date left and we think there will not be roses for us.

We are working now to expel a memory. Time is short. We thought we had all the time in the world, but now we see that time is almost up. There has been so much waiting, so much killing of time, we have become experts at killing time, but now we see we have moved through time like a cigarette's cherry, blasting matter into energy, and there's no going back. So we must hurry to expel the memory, to blow it out through the mouth and nose and pussy and asshole, all the points of exit of the body.

The last memory, the one that will accompany us as we make our peace with the needle, or the current, or just the eternity of the rooms, the jumpsuits, the ever-loving bus, is the memory of the dark moment when we made our little slip. Anyone could do it, and anyone did do it at least once or maybe even more. And what ultimately turns out to matter, against what we thought we may have believed, what in the end influences everything we will become, is what we were holding when that moment came. Was it someone's hand or a sandwich or a paintbrush or a gun? Where we were standing, what we were holding—these are the important things. More important, as it turns out, than life.

We must turn inward to that memory, the one of the bank manager, who may not in fact have been a manager, he may have been a janitor or a truck driver or nothing at all, just a man, but he would do. He did. And we realize, those petals of blood we plucked from him, those are our roses.

We will soon have to leave the bus. We take one last look in the window's reflection, a pale simulacrum our face, with some blowy trees behind. How becoming we look, how precious. Orange may be our colour after all.

Now we are ready. No one, not one of you, will ever be this elegant.

We hold tight. And then we let go.

Glory Days

Things are different now that you're in Grade 5. In Grade 4 everything was simpler, and brighter, and you had a crush on Optimus Prime. You drew hearts and kisses all over the Transformers colouring book, the ridge of your drawing hand stained ballpoint blue. If anyone came into the room you would slam the book shut, quickly but not too quickly, because the important thing about crushes is that someone knows you have one, but not that you want them to know.

Optimus Prime: sort of a man, sort of a truck, but neither one exactly, which made it okay. You knew what they meant when they said *more than meets the eye*. It meant he would know when to hold your hand, when to admire your drawings of him, when to make Brian Freeholt, that snot-nosed little bully, explode in a violet spray of gore during recess after he pantsed you and called you king of the gaylords. Which you knew was a pathetic insult because gay means happy and what's the difference between a king and a lord? Nothing. But that was Grade 4, and now it's Grade 5, and Grade 5 means *Bridge to Terabithia* and owl pellets and Western dancing and a new kind of geometry—the geometry of Bruce.

You could see it: Bruce coming home all sweaty and tired, an argument over who was going to make dinner, hurt feelings, and then maybe a make-up hug, and after that you weren't sure what would happen but just thinking about it would make you squeeze your thighs together until a strange feeling rushed up your spine.

During the height of your Optimus Prime obsession, your mom asked you one day if you wanted to see a Transformer in real life. You nodded, wondering if she could see your heart speeding up right through your shirt. She took you into the basement and showed you your grandmother's ancient sewing machine, which was bolted to a dark wooden stand. "Look," she said, lifting a flap and dropping the black iron machine into the centre of the stand, "it transforms… into a table. Pretty cool, huh?" You stared at her, considering that maybe your brother was right and she really did hate you for coming out her butthole and not her belly button the way he did.

Now you remembered that moment with affection and regret. You wished you had taken her hand and said, "Gee Mom, that is neat. We should spend some more time together." After all, you understood her better now—you too knew something of the desire for men.

Your newfound relationship with Bruce wasn't something you felt you could share, with your mother or any of the various men she brought home to meet you, or with your brother and his banger friends. Especially not them. They considered Bruce old-fashioned and kind of wimpy, preferring instead the strutting attitude and choir-girl-on-drugs shrieking of long-haired bands like KISS and Alice Cooper. The one time you tried to impress them by casually dropping the needle onto *Darkness on the Edge of Town* while they sat around the kitchen table, they snorted like pit bulls and poked fun at the album cover.

"Did this guy just fall off the back of the ugly truck? He looks like a short-order cook." Your brother snatched the needle off the turntable, tossed the record onto a bar stool, and hastily fumbled *Master of Reality* out of its sleeve. "Sorry guys, next time I'll keep the door closed."

You didn't understand what the metalheads saw in these guys—they seemed like girls dressed up for Halloween. And they weren't even pretty girls. And even if they were, what was so manly about that? Bruce wasn't pretty either, but he was something more than pretty. He reminded you of a sip of wine you had tasted from the dregs of a glass your mother left out after one of her dates. At first it made your tongue curdle in its pink bed, and you nearly spat it onto the kitchen floor, but then abruptly it changed in your mouth, ripening and spreading, until it was almost unbearably rich and full. It was nothing like the sweet, syrupy fruit drink its colour had led you to expect. It was better.

You listened to Bruce and wondered how it was possible to have already made enough mistakes to set your life growing slowly but unavoidably off-kilter, a tree planted too close to a fence, bark oozing inch by painful inch through the painted slats. That Saturday you lay on the cool floor of the basement, telephone pressed to your ear, when one of your brother's friends, a lanky kid named Aaron, passed by on his way to the downstairs bathroom. A year older than your brother, Aaron was practically an adult—he had just started Grade 9 at the school where kids smoked on the lawn, flicking ashes at cars through the wire fence. You liked the way he always wore a different brand-new Maiden shirt, as though he had an endless supply of them in the back of a truck somewhere. And maybe he did. He came from that kind of family.

You dialled the number on the back of the Smarties box, underneath where it said *Call for more information*, while listening to the water running in the bathroom and Bruce hollering about the highway and where it was going to take him.

"Nestlé Corporation," said a voice with a southern drawl.

"Hi," you said. "I'm calling for more information."

"I'm sorry?"

"Well, I'd like to get some more information. It said I could call for some on the box."

"Huh. Well is there a product you're especially interested in?"

You blanked as Aaron came out of the bathroom, drying his hands on his jeans, and saw you lying on the floor, carrying on a senseless conversation with a call centre in Arkansas or Bangalore. Aaron winked at you, then flicked some loose drops of water from his hand onto your face. "Hey fag," he said, not in a mean way. *Get a life*, you mouthed, and he smiled and blew you a kiss.

"Hello?" said the receiver, as Aaron's acid-washed-denim butt disappeared up the stairs. "Is there something in particular you're interested in?" You thought about that question until the line went dead, and after the record had spun itself out you were still there on the cool cement floor, the phone resting on your crotch and the small windows darkening.

A few weeks later you were walking down Ethelbert toward the river when you saw Aaron sitting on a bench by a bus stop. Next to him was a man about the same age as your father was the last time you saw him. He had smooth grey hair and a square, bristly chin—what your mother would call a silver fox. You lowered your eyes and kept walking, but Aaron called out to you.

"What's up?"

"Nothing."

"Just walking around?"

"Yeah," you said. The truth was you were going to look for buried treasure in the thick sticky mud-carpet the river had left after the spring flood, but somehow that wasn't something you wanted to share with Aaron.

"Cool. I like walking around too. You meet all sorts of people."

"Yeah." You looked at the toes of your sneakers, wondering when it would be okay to leave.

"Like me," said the strange man. You looked up. "That's how you met me," said the man, and Aaron rolled his eyes.

"Aren't you his dad?" you said. For the first time you noticed how much your voice sounded like Mickey Mouse's.

The man laughed. He laughed and laughed, way more laughter than necessary. Aaron didn't laugh. He smiled at you, the kind of smile that's about your mouth, not about your eyes. Then he said, "Hey, I have something for you."

"Yeah?"

"Yeah. Jerry, give the kid that thing you got at the garage sale."

"What?"

"Give it to him. He loves Springsteen."

"Well, I happen to love Springsteen too."

Aaron rolled his eyes again. "You love the idea of Springsteen. That's not the same."

"Huh," the man said. He looked cranky, but he reached into the pocket of his leather jacket and brought out a tape. *Born in the USA.*

"Thanks," you said, even though you already had it on vinyl.

For a reply the man lifted his hands and shoulders in a shrug, like he was saying *No big deal* but also *What else can I do?* "Enjoy," he said.

"See ya," said Aaron, and that meant you were done.

It turns out a cassette tape is even better for skipping than a flat rock. You gave it a few practice flings, warming up your arm, and then sent it out over the river's glimmering surface. You counted the skips. Seven.

The Shirt

I went to the party at Marty's insistence, and maybe because I had an inkling that something was going to happen. One of those psychic tingles that foreshadows a life-changing event, though generally I'm wrong about these things. When I was fifteen I had a panic attack that lasted three days—at the end of it OJ Simpson was found not guilty. I've learned to listen to the feeling in a muted way, like listening to the radio while you're doing something else, with the back of your brain. You pay attention or you don't; either way the radio is on.

"We'll make an appearance," Marty said, like we were celebrities. Marty wanted a wingman, and I was happy to oblige. The alternative was *The Wire* and two fingers of scotch. I'm not saying this in a self-pitying way. At a certain age a man gets comfortable with the alternatives he sets out for himself. But I felt like I owed Marty something, and a party—strangers, sociability, a little of the old palaver—seemed a reasonable payback.

This party seemed to have not yet gotten its sea legs. Rafts of people drifted here and here, flotsam and jetsam, drifters holding bottles by the neck. I knew fewer people than I didn't. That was becoming normal.

I noticed the shirt before I noticed who was wearing it. It was Dior, a striped button-down, aristocratic in its bold colours. Blue and gold, royal shades. I knew it was Dior because I had the same one. Not everyone can pull off a Dior shirt, and I include myself in that category. I bought it because my girlfriend at the time liked excess, in fashion at least, and I was experimenting. With what I'm not sure. Experimenting with experimenting. She and I split up and the shirt went from heavy to medium rotation. I wore it more the closer I got to laundry day. Eventually it ended up at the back of my closet, jammed in with some parkas and a Hawaiian shirt I'd thought better of. There was a cigarette burn between the third and fourth button, from when Marty tried to hug me and missed.

The guy in the shirt flitted in and out of my peripheral vision for a while. I passed him coming out of the bathroom, then he was standing in the hallway with three other guys. They seemed to be talking about a movie, but then I heard one of them say "PvP or PvE" and I realized it was a video game. Later, when I went to get another beer from the fridge, I saw him on the balcony, having a lonely cigarette. He wore no jacket, which is how I knew it was the same guy. An old girlfriend told me I was face-blind, but I'm really more man-blind. I can tell women apart easily; men, only by their hair and what they're wearing. In movies from the fifties and before I'm completely at sea—all those matching crewcuts and shirt-tie combos.

"Andrew," Marty said, appearing next to me with a girl in tow, "this is Selena. She just moved here from Beijing. Selena, Andrew used to live in China."

"Taiwan," I said.

"Exactly," Marty said.

"Where in Taiwan?" Selena asked.

"Taipei."

"For how long?"

"Two years," I said. "I was an English teacher."

"I spent some time there too, as a student," Selena said.

"Perfect!" Marty said. He scuttled off, and Selena and I got to talking about Taipei. I told her about how I taught the kids in my class to sing Johnny Cash's "Ring of Fire" more or less phonetically, and how I expected to feel awkward being over six feet tall, and never did, and how there were certain foods I still missed and couldn't find anywhere here.

"This one kind of green vegetable," I said. "I've never seen it before or since, but it was in everything. At first I hated it, but now I crave it all the time. It's been bothering me for years." I don't know why I said this, since it was something I barely thought about anymore. But talking to Selena I suddenly felt it was very important, like she was going to be the key to my gaining some kind of understanding of myself. "Do you know what I mean?" I said.

"Not really," Selena said.

"It was kind of a combination of kale, mustard and something almost soapy tasting, like cilantro maybe?"

Selena shook her head. "I don't know," she said.

"Well, anyway," I said.

"Yeah."

She smiled at me then, in this way that reminded me of my old girlfriend Jinghua. It wasn't just because she had that same accent where the consonants curve around the vowels like cupped hands. It was this quality of smile that I had always interpreted as being secretly for me—there was an outward part of it, which was to show the world that everything was going great, but it had an inner chamber too, a chamber of irony and some pleasure withheld, reserved for me only. Now I saw myself on the other side of that smile, and I wondered what had really been going on in Jinghua's head.

Some time later I ended up on a sofa with Selena, the guy in the shirt, and a couple other people. Someone had put on The Velvet Underground. Marty had gone on a dep run with the girl he was after, so things seemed to be progressing well in that department. Selena mentioned I had been an English teacher, and the guy in the shirt took that with a kind of grave interest.

"Did you like teaching English?"

"I guess I did," I said. "It's satisfying to watch people actually get better at something they'll use in life."

"What's your favourite verb tense?" he said, leaning forward with his hands on his knees. The shirt was frayed at the collar and cuffs, and had a cigarette burn between the third and fourth button.

"The present perfect," I said after a moment.

"Why?"

"It's the most difficult to explain," I said. "I don't know if it's particular to English but a lot of ESL learners have trouble with it. But once you get it, it changes how you think about time. And," I said, "it has the best name."

"Present perfect," said the girl whose apartment I think we were in.

I sneaked another look at the shirt. It fit him differently than it had me—it was longer, but tighter in the chest and shoulders. He was bulkier, like a guy who works out, or used to.

I had left for Taipei five years ago, after six months of

unemployment and binge drinking. My room was a futon and some cassette tapes. I had a TOEFL certificate and a prescription for Adderall, and I didn't much care where I ended up. I remember falling asleep in the Dior shirt the night before I left, next to a girl I'd met at the bar. In the morning she sat on the futon, naked under the shirt, drinking coffee while I frantically packed. "Do you want any of this stuff?" I asked her. "Clothes? Coffee mug? Music? I have a tape dub of *Live at the Gymnasium*." But she didn't have a cassette player. I sent her a postcard when I first got to Taiwan and we messaged a few times, and then I met Jinghua and end of story.

"What do you mean, it changes how you think about time?" the guy said.

"Well," I said, "because it doesn't describe an event that occurs at a specific point in time, like, say 'I ate a sandwich.' It's about whether or not something is part of your total life experience. 'I have eaten a sandwich.' There's no specific time at which you ate a sandwich, but sandwich-eating is something you can say you've done."

"Total life experience. That's good. I like that," the guy said.

"Lovely," said the girl whose apartment it was.

People said I was different when I came back from Taiwan, and it's true, I was. But not in the way they thought. "Andrew's been pussy-whipped," the guys said. The girls said "domesticated." It's true I didn't party the way I used to, but it wasn't that, exactly. I was like a person who finds out that his incurable, fatal disease was actually just allergies. People saw the look in my eyes, the new-found knowledge of impending life, and they mistook it for calm, or resignation. I didn't care.

We were out of beer. Marty had been gone for what

seemed like hours, and I assumed he had abandoned the party for greener pastures. This wasn't atypical of Marty. Once, back in university, he didn't show up for a dinner. We got worried, and more worried, and when we were on the verge of calling hospitals he showed up wasted, close to midnight, with an enormous hickey on his neck.

I offered to go to the dep, and the guy in the shirt said he'd come with. Someone had lined up all the Blundstones in the vestibule in ascending order of size and it took us a while to pick ours out.

"Is that shirt designer?" I said.

The guy frowned. "Yeah, I think it's Ralph Lauren or something." He said *Lauren* like he was saying a girl's name.

"Did you know Ralph Lauren's real name is Ralph Lifshitz?"

He considered, shrugging on his coat. "I think I did know that," he said. When he opened the front door a wall of cold air met us. After the close hot party it felt great. The stairs were dusted with a fine fresh layer of new snow—it must have fallen since Marty and I arrived.

"What's funny about that," I said, descending the stairs, "is how people change their name from Lipshitz to Lifshitz."

"Because it's really the lip part that gets you," he said.

"Exactly," I said, a little surprised. "We can't have people going around calling us lip-shits. I know, let's change it to *lif*."

"I had a teacher in junior high named Mrs. Holding Dicks," he said.

"No."

"Truth."

"How do you spell that?"

"H-O-L-D-E-N hyphen D-I-X."

"Get out."

"I heard lately that she shortened it. To just Dix."

"That's pretty good," I said.

"I don't think I know your name," he said.

"Andrew."

"Neil."

We walked the rest of the way to the depanneur in silence. Having told each other our names we were suddenly shy, like a couple after their first kiss. We paid for a case of beer and turned back. The snow was too powdery to crunch or even squeak—it absorbed our footsteps like heavy felt.

"Where did you get that shirt?" I said, like a guy who is just interested in men's fashion.

"Oh," he said. He made a thinking face, as though trying to look like he couldn't quite recall where the shirt had come from. "It was my ex's," he said. "She never wore it, so she gave it to me. She got it off some guy she had a thing with. She stole it from his room. She was kind of a klepto. I'm pretty sure she ripped off fifty bucks from me once." He sounded more sad than angry about it.

"What was her name?"

"Kara."

"Tara?"

"Kara."

We passed a lamppost, then another.

"That was me," I said.

"What?"

"That was me."

"What was you?"

"The guy. The thing. The guy she took the shirt from. That was my shirt."

Neil looked at me. He seemed about to say something, then changed his mind. "You want it back?" he finally said.

"No, man. It's yours."

We were back at the apartment. Neil more or less jogged up the stairs, the bottles clanking against each other in the box. As I was taking off my boots in the hallway I could hear Marty's complaining voice from the kitchen.

"What the hell? I said I'd be ten minutes!"

"Sorry," I said, taking off my coat and draping it overtop an open door. "We didn't think you were coming back."

Marty was offended at that. "You could have texted," he said.

"'Yo dawg you in the bone zone or what?'"

He tilted his head, considering this. "Unlikely," he said. "She was all 'I have to get the last metro.'"

"Bummer."

"Women, amiright?"

We clinked bottles.

"So what about Selena?" he said. "You all up on that?"

"I comported myself like a perfect gentleman."

"What, too good for her or something?"

"I'm not exactly on the market," I said. "But I appreciate the gesture."

He squinted at me. "You need to move on," he said. "You know what my dad says."

I did.

"'The only way to get over someone is to get under some-one.'"

"I know," I said. "Thanks."

"Whatever." He shuffled off into the living room. I put my fingers over my eyes and pressed. When I took them away again Neil was standing in front of me. He seemed to be at the centre of a deep red aura. After a few moments it cleared.

"You smoke?" he said.

"Quit," I said.

"Good on ya." He stepped out onto the balcony. I followed. "I could use some fresh air," I said. Neil nodded.

"How long were you with Kara?"

"A year," he said. "A year and change."

I nodded, trying not to seem surprised, though I was.

"Are you... Do you still see her around?"

For an answer he lifted his half-full bottle of beer to his mouth and drank it off in one continuous gulp. Then he set it down on the balcony railing, carefully and with some finality. He smiled a closed-mouth smile and went inside.

His cigarette was still burning so I picked it up and took a drag. I remembered something from an Ian Fleming novel. *The drink Bond enjoyed the most was the drink he had in his head, before the first drink of the day.* I guess Fleming knew something about something.

The door opened again and Neil came back out, wearing a puffy nylon jacket. His face was composed but he seemed inflamed, excited somehow, like something under his skin was jumping around in there.

"Sorry about that," he said. He cleared his throat. "The thing about it is, Kara died. I mean she's dead. So no, I don't really see her around. Though actually that's not true. I actually see her around all the time. You know? Like I'll see some girl on the street or something, and for a second I'll think, hey, there's Kara, or I'll be on the bus and suddenly I'll, you know, smell her smell, and suddenly it's like she's right there, you know what I mean?"

"Yeah," I said.

"But it's not her."

"No," I said.

"Fuck," he said. "I'm sorry. I'm being so selfish right now.

I'm sorry you had to find out like this."

"It's okay," I said. "I didn't know her well."

"She was alright," he said tightly, and I realized he was trying not to cry. I patted his shoulder a couple times and went back inside.

In the bathroom I looked up Kara's Facebook page. It took a little while because I couldn't remember her last name. When I found it, I saw it had become a memorial site, like those heaped flowers you see sometimes alongside a highway.

MISSING U

<3U 4EVR

<3<3<3

Hey Kara thought of you today miss you big time girl

LOVE U

<3

They were old messages; the most recent one was dated last spring, about the time Jinghua and I broke up for the last time.

Someone knocked on the door.

"Just a minute," I said.

Once Jinghua and I took the bullet train out to a small fishing village whose name I forget. We had an idea about picnicking in nature, but we couldn't seem to find it. We walked through three or four villages, each time expecting the buildings to thin out and nature to encroach, until we found the bank of a small creek or a wooded hill to spread our blanket on, but each village just blended into the next. It was spring, a day that would have been considered glorious by Quebec standards, but cold for Taiwan. Jinghua shivered in her light jacket. After an hour of walking we decided to head back to the station, buy lunch there and save our picnic for another day. We took a bridge over a river, which was full and fast that time of year. "Let's drop our plates into the river and see whose gets to the other side of the bridge first," I suggested. I marked my plate with an *X* and hers with an *O*, and we counted to three and dropped them, then ran to other side of the bridge and waited for the plates to appear. We were both laughing like kids. "Go plate go," Jinghua shouted. The wind whipped her hair around and I thought I would never feel as much love for her as I did at that moment.

And it was true, I never did. Even though we stayed together for almost three years, including one excruciating year of long distance and that disastrous spring she spent in Montreal, the spring we broke up, and even though I loved her more completely and fully than any other person I have known, and that includes my family, that time on the bridge was the peak of it, my maximum output of love. Of course I didn't know it at the time. Would it have been better if I did?

The snow had started again sometime during the night. The footprints, mine and Neil's, were almost totally obscured now, and I lost track of them a block from the party. My old MP3 player had a radio receiver and so I put that on. The CBC's overnight programming, those voices that are just barely foreign: Dutch, South African, the crumbling Empire. A report on go-kart racing, some oldies music. Fats Domino singing "Blueberry Hill". And suddenly I found that what I had thought to be a thickness was actually a thinness, the icing on a layer cake of sadness I had forgotten was there. Those warm blueberries, that lonely hill. I telescoped out, feeling amazed and very old, remembering all the sadness I'd felt more or less since adulthood, and sometimes before. There was a lot, a whole flea market of sadnesses. And yet the biggest sadness there, the piece that throbbed and glowed like a shard of uranium, that piece wasn't mine.

The Polar Bear at the Museum

I n gym class we have to measure ourselves with callipers to find out how much of our body is made up of pure fat, as if we are bags of microwave popcorn. You are supposed to pinch a wodge of skin between the callipers' ends, measuring your belly, thighs, upper arms, all the mayonnaise-coloured hairless bits. The thickness of the roll of flesh you conjure up tells you how much of you consists of dimpled subcutaneous lard and how likely you are to die young.

Beth says the callipers look like something from the museum of gynecology. She squeezes her entire bicep, her neck, encircles her head with the metal jaw, placing each end in her ear like a stethoscope, taking down measurements as she goes. Her body-fat percentage comes out to ninety-eight. I try to imagine her carved out of butter, two scornful coffee-bean eyes pressed into the head.

Beth is the smartest one, and the funniest. Also the meanest. Hugging her is like embracing a deck of cards, all flat bone and thin edges you could cut yourself on. She likes to talk about beating up Trina James after school, even though Trina is usually scheduled to fight Morgan Fernandez, who wears a tiny crucifix around her neck and has sad sepia-coloured eyes. Trina also wears a crucifix but she has buck teeth and bushy eyebrows. We hate her because she is almost as ugly as we are.

Trina asks if we will get her back in the fight. "Why don't you grow some more teeth to cover up those gums," says Beth.

Beth and I play outfield so we can smoke behind the bleachers by the racetrack. We don't have cigarettes, but we roll dried bits of things in paper and set them on fire, then lean over and huff the smoke until we feel giddy. Being in the "gifted" class means nobody cares if you can't throw a curveball or run to second base without getting winded, so we hide out until it's time to change back into our plaid-and-corduroy uniforms and throw our big brains around.

We have to take gym class with the regular kids so we don't become conceited or soft. Corey Kowalchuk is a regular kid, and so pretty it makes you sad just to look at him and think about how in forty years he'll either be ugly or dead. One time he tells Beth that Mitch Lewis, who is sitting next to him on the workout bench, has a crush on her, and that he jerks off about her every night with the telephone in his hand and calls her just before he comes. Mitch just stares at his white Adidas that look like small spacecraft. Next Corey turns to me and tells me in a bored-sounding voice that Mitch Lewis wants to hump me, but his dick is too small so he's going to tie a broomstick to it and do me until I'm torn and bleeding. Mitch continues to look at his sneakers, a furious grin on his face. I am secretly excited that Corey has spoken to me this much.

Corey's parents live down the street from mine, and back in elementary school we used to take the school bus together to the public school downtown, because our parents didn't want to send us to the private school in our neighbourhood in case we grew up to be assholes. We used to sit together at the back of the bus in our DayGlo snowsuits and make up stupid jokes about our teachers. One time the school bus hit a massive pothole, and our tiny little kid bodies bounced really high up off the seats, and both of us swore to each other that we could feel the roof of the schoolbus brushing the stiff hair at the top of our heads. A few years after that Corey started getting high at recess, and I started wearing a bra and listening to musicals, and we mostly stopped talking to each other, unless Corey has some junior-high wastoid like Mitch Lewis he wants to humiliate. I guess this is something we learned about in Life Skills class, though I don't remember anything except Ms. Jablonsky putting a condom on a banana.

Trina James may or may not be a slut, but we know for sure that Mary Roberts is. We can tell because she wears short skirts and knee socks and laughs at boys' jokes. Also, she has baby teeth. These teeth clearly belong in the mouth of a precocious eight-month-old, they are fit only for chewing boiled carrots and celery stew, and yet here they are, lining Mary's gums like seed pearls sewn onto red velvet. BJ teeth, Beth calls them, and we all laugh and pretend to know what she means.

Beth is one gutsy lady. That is what Mrs. Chernyk, the art teacher, says when Beth refuses to snap her gum even though Janine Raymond, the school bully, tells her she has to. Janine enjoys the sound of snapping gum and forces entire classes of terrified kids to do it in unison. Beth just glares at her and bares her teeth, which makes her look like an angry koala bear. Janine tells Beth she will beat her up after school, as soon as Beth is done blowing the janitor, her alleged favourite activity. Mary Roberts snickers, her head bowed over a pencil drawing of Teemu Selänne scoring a goal. *Go Jets!!!!!!!* it says at the bottom, in letters that look like bolts of lightning. You're next, Roberts, says Janine, and Mary hunches down with her HB pencil and busily starts adding about thirty more exclamation points to her caption. Beth turns slightly and gives me this warm and reassuring smile, like I'm the one about to get the living crap beat out of her by a girl with STAY DOWN tattooed on her knuckles.

I stand by Beth's locker at 3:30, sober and brave and so full of resigned, heartsick love I think I am going to rupture. We wait for Janine to appear and curb-stomp Beth into martyrdom with her purple Doc Martens, but Janine never shows up. My devotional ardour deflates into shame, like a run-over volleyball. After all, I snapped my gum along with the rest of them.

You don't even really need to pay to see the bison at the Museum. They're right there in the lobby, their great heavy heads all full of sawdust and Excelsior and old sweaters. You can stand there all day and stare at them for free. Which is exactly what Beth is trying to do. Our class is supposed to be researching lichens of the Canadian Shield, but so far Beth hasn't even made it past the ticket booth. She is moored to the parquet floor, leaning against our side of the velvet rope like she's waiting to be let into the Oscars, looking.

The bison are mounted mid-charge, glass eyes peering over their shoulders in what I guess is supposed to be terror, running from a group of two-dimensional aboriginal hunters on horseback who are painted on the wall behind them.

Mary Roberts saunters by and glances at us. "Hey, check it out," she says, "Beth has a boyfriend. Dances With Retards hump'um Big Chief Saggenballs." I wait for Beth to spit out some insult or slap Mary's face, but she just stands there, looking kind of pathetic. Mary laughs and bounces away.

"God," says Beth, "you wonder why they didn't just find some real Indians to stuff." Her voice is flat and empty of bitterness.

Beth's dad gets reincarnated every now and then into different bodies, depending on her mood. Sometimes he's a Mennonite, a peacenik who wriggled through the border in the sixties, the ashes of his draft card still warm in his pocket, who was then tucked away by her mother's church group. This story is for when Beth and I are lying on her bed, our eyes red from the joint we've finally learned how to smoke. Her voice when she tells it is soft and dreamy, with none of the corrosive acid that's usually there.

When the combination of asbestos insulation and mouse droppings in the church's basement set off florid rashes and welts on the young draft dodger's skin, Beth's mother set up a cot in her own basement and offered him whatever semblance of Christian charity she could muster. He thanked her, sneezing and wiping his oozing eyes on a handkerchief embroidered with tiny clocks.

During the day Beth's mother would run the church group's printing press, turning out pamphlets on the importance of hard work, faith and chastity, and at night she would bring chamomile tea to the runaway and they'd discuss their views on the war and the intricacies of their respective faiths. Pretty soon cups of tea became candle-lit dinners eaten off tin camping dishes, and the young Menno, who in Beth's stories looked a lot like Keanu Reeves, fell in love with the Catholic woman. Although she loved him too, his minky black hair and carpentry skills, Beth's mother couldn't picture herself married to this man who didn't dance, but who sang like an angel, and loved round wood-hewn buildings, free of dusky corners where cobwebs and secrets flourished. Neither of them was willing to compromise, and the word *chastity* floated over their relationship, a naphthalene-smelling ghost. After a few months of whispered fights and unbreakable dishes thrown across the room, the draft dodger left for a rural commune in Saskatchewan. Beth's mother threw herself into her work at the printing press, and though her faith in the Holy Trinity was fading, she found comfort in the smell of mimeograph ink.

She heard nothing from the draft dodger for years, until one evening he appeared on her doorstep. I don't have much time, he said, they found me. I've been court martialled. Tomorrow I'm being smuggled to Paraguay. He still looked like Keanu Reeves, though his hair was longer and straggly and streaky-grey. She let him in. What else could she do? He left early the next morning in a white van with Alaskan plates, and Beth's mother never heard from him again.

"And nine months later," Beth finishes, "I was born."

"Wait a second," I say, "President Carter pardoned the draft dodgers in 1977, so he couldn't have been in real trouble." (I'm not the Reach for the Top regional team captain for nothing.)

"Yeah, sure," says Beth, "but you had to apply for a pardon, and there was a time limit anyway. He never got his."

"Why wouldn't he apply?" I ask.

"I don't know, because he was getting high on some fucking commune, okay?"

I am silent, and Beth slowly exhales a kite's tail of smoke.

"Anyway," Beth goes on. "You know what the moral is?"

"No."

A trace of hydrochloride seeps back into her voice. "You haven't had a night until you've had a Mennonite."

The other father is for parties when Beth has smoked two or three joints and drunk most of the vodka we smuggled from my parents' liquor cabinet. "You're totally DRONED!" Mary Roberts shrieks, then laughs hysterically, the silver wig she's wearing making funny shushing sounds. Beth scowls at her, then grabs Mary's hand and jams it against her belly, poking two of Mary's fingers against what looks like an appendectomy scar.

"Feel that?" Beth says quietly, while Mary giggles. "That was a present from my dad. You know what his name was, right? Big Chief Saggenballs."

"Ow," says Mary, wriggling out of Beth's grasp. "God, you're so *intense*."

The first time Beth and I take mushrooms we lie on her bedroom floor and stare at the ceiling spackle for as long as our scorched eyes can stand. My face feels hot and huge, my cheeks two knobs of burning fat. The air has resolved itself into a series of churning interlocked pinwheels, which for some reason appear only in crimson and ecru, our school's team colours. I want to tell Beth about this but my throat has telescoped out about ten feet from my body and it's so hard to get the words through to my mouth. Besides, she is thumbing through a copy of *Maclean's* and laughing quietly to herself, and I don't want to disturb her.

Later we go to the social club near Beth's house and play the Freddy Krueger pinball game, pummelling the flipper buttons before the ball gets anywhere near them and laughing shrilly when it tumbles into the game over slot. "Good FRIGHT, sleep TIGHT, don't let the bedbugs BITE," Freddy Krueger says, his voice coming out in a series of digital squirts.

"I am *so high*," whispers Beth.

Walking home we try not to step on each others' shadows. Mine looks absurdly tall and wobbly, like old cartoons of trees in the desert or hula dancing giraffes. "I'm a giraffe," I say, my chest already collapsing with despair at how completely lame this sounds. Instead of dissolving the ego, as they are supposed to do, the mushrooms have turned me into a feedback loop of agonizing self-consciousness. I feel like a failure, even as a stoner.

When we get back to the house Beth's mother is in the kitchen listening to a Pete Seeger tape. "Did you have a nice night, girls?" she asks. My head feels emptied out and tender, and there is Beth, disappearing up the staircase without even a look in my direction. I whisper goodnight to her mother and stumble over the carpeted stairs. We fall asleep on our backs but somehow in the night we turn like magnets, and when I wake up early in the morning I am spooning her, my hand against her ribs, and I can feel her heart beating as surely as if I held it, bald and leaping, in my palm.

The polar bear at the museum lives in a glass display case in the entrance hallway to the museum, frozen in a state of boredom following a seal kill. The taxidermied seal, twice dead, lies some distance away, the bear apparently uninterested in its quarry. Behind the bear's shoulder the fibre-optic sky goes from light blue to royal blue to black and back to light blue again in quick succession. Sometimes in the artificial night sky the aurora borealis appears, a green ghost dragging across the wall. In this hallway the sound of the north wind is always blowing.

A Goddamn Fucking Cake

If we don't get to Alicia's Yule party on time we'll miss the gift exchange. I could give a crap, but Alicia is shrill and if we're late she's liable to break an eardrum. Bruce doesn't need that, not now. Cody's already asleep in his crib; I kiss him goodbye and tell Rebecca to put her circuit kit away when she's finished with it. She rolls her eyes. Premature adolescence: those hormones in the water, the plastics we use, et cetera. I give the sitter the lowdown and go out to the car. Bruce is already there, head leaning against the window, a blanket spread over his knees. He's always cold since the chemo.

"Ready to rock and roll?" I say. He smiles. In his head he's teasing me about the way I talk, an old fart's self-conscious stab at coolness, but he's too tired to say it out loud. He's become quieter, more thoughtful—he was always gentle and shy, but he's also clever, with a fast sharp tongue, and lately he seems like he's been slowed and softened. *Chemo brain*, I read somewhere, and then wished I hadn't.

"All right," I say, "let's boogaloo."

Alicia has thrown this Yule party for the past five years, as long as we've known her, and it's always on the same day, December 15th. Right after the term lets out, but before everyone becomes swept up in family visits and excessive consumption. A chance for the teachers to cut loose a little, socialize outside the offices where we toss back grainy instant and gripe to each other over the whir of the photocopier.

Alicia prides herself on throwing a hell of a shaker. All of our colleagues will be there, and due to the shape of our lives lately that also constitutes all of our friends. I'd happily stay home and give myself a root canal, but Bruce gets out so seldom. It was he who pushed me to go, this despite the fact that he looks more or less unconscious against the car window. A faint white smear of condensation grows and shrinks where his breath comes out. Touch wood.

Alicia lives in a condo in the hip part of town, an old immigrant neighbourhood that's now populated by artists and students, the streets bursting with cafés, health food stores, tiny bistros that offer two kinds of veggie sandwich and spicy lentil sludge. It smells pleasingly of bagels on Sunday afternoons.

Alicia teaches media studies and is considered by most of the staff to be postmodern and vaguely radical. She has her students keep "spin diaries" where they record evidence of attempted brainwashings, and teaches a unit on culture jamming. She's a respected young teacher, full of energy and spark, a firecracker, and her students adore her. Which is easy when your class consists of internet videos and looking at airbrushed models all day. I don't resent her, not really. But organic chemistry is not the kind of subject that ignites a teenager's will to live. I try to make it fun for them, bring in tropical fruit snacks when we do the aromatics, show them the compound structures for caffeine and

THC, but they only care what's on the exam.

Parking in this neighbourhood requires an aeronautics degree from MIT, but after twenty minutes I manoeuvre into a spot that won't be too far a walk for Bruce. I start to get out to open his door but then I remember.

"Wait a sec, hon," I say. I reach into the back seat and pull out a flat box marked *Ogilvy* that's tied with a curly gold ribbon. I hand it to him.

"Bernie," he says. My students call me Bernie too, or Mrs. Bernie, which is funny but better than Bernadette and especially better than Mrs. Faber-Watson.

"It's a cashmere scarf," I say, "and don't make a big deal out of it because it sucks, I know it does. You deserve better. You deserve a fucking castle on the Rhine, but you're getting a cashmere scarf so just shut up about it already."

Bruce smiles and takes my hand. "How did I come to deserve a wife as terrible as you," he says.

"God only knows. Happy birthday, monster."

"I love you," he says. We kiss. His lips are dry and cold.

For five years now Alicia has held her Yule party on Bruce's birthday, co-opting all our colleagues and stuffing them so full of booze and canapés that they're too hungover and bloated for the next week to think about having cocktails or even macaroni and cheese with Bruce and me. And Bruce has never said a thing to her about it, because he's too sweet and self-effacing. He says he doesn't care, but it chafes me, even though I've never said anything either. Of course she knows it's his birthday, everyone knows, and every year at the party he gets back-patted and toasted and maybe even handed a trinket or two from his closer friends in the department, but the party is really and ultimately about Alicia and her gorgeous condo, her sound system and whatever DJ she's hired for the night, her snack trays with local organic gluten-free ingredients, as Alicia tells us repeatedly, Alicia and her superhuman ability to be smart and toned and a great teacher and a volunteer at the Immigrant Workers' Centre and still somehow have time and resources to throw The Party of the Millennium (So Far!).

I slam the door too hard after I help Bruce out and he jumps a little. "Relax, kid, you're makin me nervous," he says. I take his hand and we walk up the outdoor staircase together, which is treacherous with snow. When we get to the door Bruce hums the Death Star theme. He is rallying, for my sake. As happens about every three days, my chest is crushed by a suffocating love for him, a love like a giant fist that squeezes my lungs into pancakes. I fight it, because if I don't I will cry, or hit someone.

There is a shriek from the hallway, and Alicia rushes at us, a gale of scarves and tinkling silver bracelets and a sweet jasmine smell. I shriek back and we hug. "Bernadette, you are the mostest," she says. "You look fan*ta*bulous."

"I am ravishing, aren't I?" I say.

Then she turns to Bruce and hugs him tightly, not put off by his frailty, for which I'm grateful, though I worry she might snap a rib. "You look great," she says.

"Alicia, you mendacious bitch," I say, "he looks like shit and you know it."

"Hi Alicia," Bruce says, smiling at the floor. "It's nice to see you."

"It's nice to be seen. How about you kids put your coats in the bedroom, and then head over to the kitchen and let me fix you a drinkie-poo? We're about to start the gift swap."

The gift swap has complicated rules in which presents are taken from a pile, but if you don't like the present you've got, you can forcibly "trade" with someone else, even if they don't want to give up their own gift. "So," says a thin blond man in a sweater-vest, "it's a 'trade' the way Canada 'traded' with the Indigenous peoples." There is some laughter. Alicia points to the man, smiling, then taps the side of her nose. I wonder if she's sleeping with him. Someone like her could have her pick, and not just among the teachers. Though maybe that's unfair—she can't be as sure-footed and brassy as she seems. Can she? For all that's said about contemporary women's sexual freedom and broad-ranging, uncrimped lust, surely some of those old demons must still stalk the female libido. Fear. Shame. Pride.

My contribution to the gift swap is a sandwich, which I made myself. I took no small amount of pains with this sandwich. It's goat cheese and grilled tofu—vegetarian-friendly—with roasted red peppers and homemade arugula pesto, on fresh pumpernickel from the Première Moisson. It's stuck with a frilled toothpick and wrapped in Saran Wrap. It might seem silly but it's bound to bring more joy than whatever Dollarama paperweights or coffee mugs are hidden in the pile. But when its recipient—a young woman who teaches, I think, videography, opens it, she looks puzzled. I explain what it is, and when I get to goat cheese she yelps "Hello, vegan!" and lunges for a stapler shaped like a hippopotamus. This stapler turns out to be the most coveted prize in the heap, and at one point a man named Martin, one of Bruce's more admired colleagues in the history department, refuses to yield it to a usurper. The two arm wrestle for it, Martin emerges the victor, hands in the air like Muhammad Ali, and when the game is over I've ended up with my own sandwich. I laugh in what I hope is a good-natured manner and put it in my purse.

Bruce sits the game out. He looks pale but he's laughing along with everyone else. "You and your goat cheese," he whispers, catching my wrist.

"Worse than Hitler," I whisper back, and he giggles.

"Let's get DOWN!" someone shouts, and whatever comes after is drowned in a surge of bass beats and swelling synth.

The condo, which was once a hat factory, is open-concept; the only true door is the bathroom's. On the way there I pass through the bedroom, and without really meaning to, I stop to examine the wall, which is hung with framed things. There are Alicia's degrees, and photos of her hiking in Thailand and receiving an award for outstanding achievement in teaching. There are a few arty black-and-white shots of buildings, and an old-fashioned drawing of a bird.

In the centre of the collection, in a plain black frame, is a portrait of three. I don't know why I've never noticed it before; it doesn't look new. Two are middle-aged women, both heavy-set. One wears a black leather jacket over a white T-shirt and has very short hair, with bangs spiking up from her forehead. Her arm is around the other woman, whose neck is draped with a colourful scarf. She has a taffy-coloured bob, and wears a touch of peach lipstick and dangly silver earrings. Her head is angled slightly towards the leather-clad woman, her mouth open as though laughing. The first woman is more stoic, but the corners of her mouth lift like she's just made a joke that satisfies her. Behind and to the left of them is a battered Suzuki motorcycle.

In between the two women is an unattractive girl of about twelve or thirteen. Her hair is long and greasy and parted in the middle. It swags over her eyes, which gaze out of the picture from behind large frameless glasses. She wears an ugly, pilled turquoise zip-up jogging sweater. Her cheeks and forehead are livid with acne, her expression one of misery unadulterated. Other than the hair and the acne, she is the spit image of the leather-clad woman.

Behind me come footsteps and I trot into the bathroom, careful not to slam the door. The knob jiggles.

"Just a minute!" I sing out.

"Get a move on, Bernie, I have to piss like a wildebeest," says the girl from the picture.

Pink grapefruit martini in hand, I swerve through the crowd like an icebreaker navigating glacial seas. An elbow pops out and jostles me, and half the drink spills onto my wrist. I find Bruce and Alicia being talked at by a young man with thick black hair that's short in front and longer on the crown of his head, where it sticks up in a brave thatch. The effect is that of the top of a pineapple. As he talks he bobs his head continuously. I hand the drink to Bruce and lick my damp forearm.

"*Labyrinth* is basically about development of female sexuality," he is saying, "the journey from child to woman, with an emphasis on the normative motherhood role." He gives me a short nod and goes on. "See, at first Sarah rejects the nurturing role she's been given over her brother. She's still a child, essentially genderless, and she just wants to play. But by the end of the movie she's come to accept and even love caring for the baby. It's reinforced continually. Hoggle, for instance, represents the male phallus, which at first is revolting to the girl-child—she finds him ugly, crude, and useless. But by the end of the movie she's made him her closest friend."

"So *Labyrinth* teaches girls to love cock," Alicia says. She looks at me and goggles her eyes. I picture that teenage girl, vulnerable as an eyelid. I widen my eyes back and mouth "shameless" at her. She smiles and pinches my side, under my bra.

"I'm making a film about it," the man says. "A documentary. I haven't started working on it yet, but the ideas are all up there." He bobs his head a few more times, to show us where the ideas are.

"I'm sorry," says Alicia. "Bernie, this is Oliver—he's a new hire in the department. Very up-and-coming. Oliver, this is Bernie. The rock of the chemistry department."

"Sounds like crystal meth," I say.

"Now there's an idea," says Bruce. "Turn the chemistry department into a meth lab. No more funding problems."

"New microscopes for everyone."

"Solid gold Bunsen burners."

"Swarovski crystal test tubes."

"That's the ticket," says Bruce.

"Speaking of," Alicia says. She takes a long rectangular tin out of her pocket; it bears the image of a lion-haired woman in a position of repose on a divan. Alicia opens the tin and takes out a copper-coloured pipe. Under the pipe is a baggie containing a spiky white substance.

"Where did you get that," says the blond sweater-vest, whose name is Jeff. The videographer is behind him, looking raptly over his shoulder.

"I know a guy," says Alicia.

"I bet she does." Bruce looks at me and I realize I've spoken out loud, though quietly.

When Alicia flames the rock there's a smell of burning

plastic. I take only a quick hit, to unbend the edges. Bruce does too. In this way we are beholden to Alicia, and she to us.

"Put some hurt on it," says Oliver as Bruce passes him the pipe. "Oh yeah, put some hurt on it."

Alicia goes to the stereo system and chooses a record. John Prine and Nanci Griffith. As a kid in Abitibi I thought John Prine was a friend of my dad's, that country music was about us.

"Alicia."

"Hnh."

"Alicia."

"What."

"You always forget."

"What."

"Every year. You always forget."

"Forget what?"

"Today," I say, "is Bruce's birthday."

"Ah," she says. "Shit. Bruce?"

Bruce shrugs in a no-denying-it-now kind of way.

"You know that," I say. "You've known that every year. But you don't care. Because your party is the mo-*host* important." As I say this I realize I am making a speech, so I try to do it up a little by standing on the futon and raising my arms in the air. And a one and a two and a—

I tell her her parties are insufferable displays of ego. I tell her she only acts sensitive and socially-aware because it looks good on her c.v., and that if she really cared about her friends she'd give a rat's ass about a man who almost died—I say it, died—and at least get him a goddamn fucking birthday cake.

I say that a shitty childhood is no excuse for such two-facedness, and what does she think, she's the only one who ever had gay moms? Suck it up.

I tell her, more or less, that she doesn't deserve Bruce's friendship, nor to a lesser extent, mine.

"But here we are," I say. "Here we goddamn fucking are."

My point made, I sit back down with a flounce. Bruce, in his infinite modesty, refuses to look at either of us.

There is a pause. Then Alicia convulses as though she's been stabbed. "Oh. My. God. Bernie. You're right. It's Bruce's *birthday*." Hands on his skinny shoulders, she leans in close. "Bruce," she says, "I'm glad you're not dead."

"Thank you, Alicia."

"Although. Please. Inquiring minds want to know."

"Yes?"

"Where *is* your other testicle?"

Someone, the videographer, issues a single barking laugh. I don't know where to put my eyes.

"I mean," Alicia continues, "they did take it off, right? Did you keep it?"

Bruce looks at his hands, his index fingers forming a steeple. Then he says "well, I had originally planned to donate it to science."

"Really? I mean, you didn't want to keep it? As a souvenir?"

"And deprive modern science of one of the great marvels of our time?"

"The Ball of Bruce," Alicia says reverently.

"Schoolchildren would come from miles around," he says. "But actually, I keep it in a jar of formaldehyde. On the mantel above the fireplace."

"*Mais non*," says Alicia.

"Saving for a special occasion," I say, somehow.

"On an unrelated note," Bruce says, "Alicia, when's *your* birthday?" Alicia laughs, throwing her head back in delight.

Some of the tension in my throat unknots, leaving only a dry ache from the smoke. I put my arm around Bruce. "I believe," I say, "the time has come for a song." He glances at me, then away again. I would do anything for him, anything. I turn to the room and raise my arm like I'm holding a baton. "And a one and a two and a—"

Mon cher ami
C'est à ton tour
De te laisser parler d'amour

The Québecois national anthem is sung in unison, and then in a round, with me conducting like Mickey Mouse in an old cartoon. A few people sing the birthday song in English, and underneath John Prine is still strumming his sad cowboy song. People sway and swing their glasses, bottles in the air, stomping on the ground, whistling and hollering at my husband. I lean in close to Bruce and sing in his ear. His face is flushed and he's staring at the floor. My dearest, my heart.

My dear friend
It's now your turn
To let yourself speak of love
Such a wonderfully simple wish.

I lift my head. I must have fallen asleep; there is a small damp spot on the upholstery where my mouth has rested. Alicia is seemingly comatose on Jeff's lap; he is mumbling the top of her head with half-conscious kisses. Bruce is gone. I run my hands through my hair a few times and hoist myself off the sofa. My eyes feel like feet and my feet feel like basketballs. I can't find Bruce anywhere in the apartment. I go into the kitchen and rinse two cigarette butts out of a glass jar, fill it with water and drink it in one go. A breeze nudges my bare ankles, and I see the door to the balcony is open a crack. Bruce is standing in the light snow, bundled in a fleece blanket, looking out across the alleyway. I slip my feet into a pair of rubber boots by the door and join him. It's cold enough. The windows of the apartments across the way are all dark.

"You doing okay?" I ask.

"Fine," he says, and continues to stare out at the alley.

"I know," I say after a moment, "but it's not her fault. She's just kind of socially retarded is all."

He looks at me, and I realize he isn't upset at Alicia. He's angry. At me, for what I did for him. To him. Furious. He could kill me with his pale skinny hands.

"Bruce," I say.

"You had no right," he says. "I hate that kind of thing. You know I do."

"I thought," I said, "I mean after everything that's happened—"

He laughs, bitterly. In that laugh I hear the old smoke, the old fire.

"Sometimes, Bernie," he says, "I wish it was you instead of me."

"You have no idea," I say. We both wait for me to say something else. The snow keeps up like it has somewhere to be.

I know what I'll do when I get home. I'll go into the baby's room. I'll stand over the crib where he's sleeping and lift him into my arms. He'll stretch a bit and moan, but he won't wake up. I'll sit in the rocking chair by the window and look out at the tree. It will be still and dark and tree-like. I would do anything for him, anything, but never the right thing, and the weight of the baby's head against my arm will be almost heavy as that knowledge, but not heavy enough.

The Yoga Teachers

Risa's mother tries for what seems like hours to get Risa's thick bumpy hair into a French braid. The hair is remarkably resistant, though Risa's mother uses a snagging angry-toothed comb, thirty-seven bobby pins, and half a jar of Dippity-do. "Ow," Risa says every time her mother pokes a bobby pin into the damp sticky mass. Her hair stands in gelled ridges over her head, like an aerial photo of the badlands. Finally, when Risa and her mother are both near tears, Risa's father knocks on the door, and Risa must get into the car with him and be driven through the long snowy corridor to her dance class.

Every week it's like this, the vinyl floor that lifts at the corners like old slices of cheese and Risa's teacher who is too beautiful, with breasts like long, smooth loaves inside her unitard, and her heavy circling arms. First position, second position, fourth position. *Bras bas*, which Risa knows is French for "arms lowered" but still thinks of as *bra-BAH*, a rallying cry shouted by staunch men on horseback as they ride into battle. First position hums like a calm day in an open field. Second position is a loud embarrassed relative. Third position is a mythological creature, half soldier and half clamshell. Fourth position is grey and ticking like the inside of a watch. Fifth position might be a little bit magic because of the way your thighs squeeze together.

Risa was not meant for ballet, this she knows. She knows it's because of the shape of her head and her thick, bumpy hair. Other girls—like tiny, flexible Shauna—have neat gravity-defying buns that rest comfortably on the back curve of their skulls. Their buns stay done up without hair nets or Dippity-do, they don't have greasy braids crunchy with bobby pins. Their heads are streamlined and aerodynamic. They look like small fighter planes, doing *grand jetés* across the floor. In comparison, Risa feels like a wooden cart or a wheelbarrow; creaky, unstable, about to crush someone's toe. Her teacher rolls her eyes when she thinks Risa isn't looking, then puts her in the back row.

This week, though, Risa's fat, beautiful, cruel teacher is not there. Instead there are a man and a woman who are here to teach them yoga. The man is blond and tanned and muscular, but he is not a babe the way her friends talk about babes like David Hasselhoff. His hair is dry and tufted, and he wears a purple sleeveless shirt out of which his arms dangle like braided rope. The woman is small and intense, with an oily nose and torn blue sweatpants. They are American, so they can't pronounce the last names of the kids in her class: Jurczak, Konwalchuk, Jzojzofsky. The yoga teachers want Risa to concentrate on her breath. Her breath is a retractable column like a telescope, and she has to push and pull it around her chest like a toy on a stick. She never knew this before, but she can see that it's true, because sometimes it sticks in her neck, where part of the column must have rusted. The woman demonstrates the proper way to inhale and exhale, and her breath echoes through her as though her chest were an underground parking lot.

The yoga teachers tell her to do strange and impossible things, like lift her heart. "Soften your lungs." "Soften your eyes." "Open your chest." Risa pictures her chest opening like the cabinet where her parents keep the good china, her guts stacked like plates and her softened lungs sitting on top like a matched pair of teacups. The man leans over Risa and murmurs into her ear, "Find your breath," and suddenly Risa feels a wash of energy move through her legs. The man has a long, gentle face like a horse. Do he and the woman do it together, opening their chests and lifting their hearts? Risa cannot imagine it. The woman seems another animal entirely, a musky and active one, like a ferret. Risa closes her eyes against these thoughts and focuses on the column of her breath turning over and over in her glass-cabinet torso.

After class Risa walks across the parking lot to her dad's car. She can still hear the rasp of the woman's breathing and her voice saying, "soften, soften, soften." Her eyes feel blunt and smooth as fingertips. She floats to the car on waves of breathing, so light and serene and feelingless, and she senses that the expression has slipped off her face like a plate of leftovers dumped into the garbage. She slides into the passenger seat and straps herself in silently. "What," her dad says. "What is it now?"

"Nothing," she says, feeling that peace and goodwill must be flowing from her in waves.

"For godsakes," her dad says, turning the ignition, "what are you upset about this time? Maybe it's time to think about quitting these classes, all they do is make you miserable."

Risa feels her soft heart fold in on itself. Her face changes from radiant to sullen, but nobody can tell the difference.

Wellspring

I have a guilty secret. The secret is that no matter what happens, there lives inside me a bright sliver of joy. It's like a hum from a machine that won't turn off. However bad things get, however hopeless or sad I feel, there it is: *zzzmmmmmmmmm*.

I've done many things to try to find the switch to quiet it. For years I volunteered as a counsellor at a drop-in centre for teens downtown. There I would hear stories of kids pricked by stray needles as they foraged for food in dumpsters, girls pregnant from gang rapes and unable to procure abortions, rampant diabetes in a thirteen-year-old boy that left him missing both his feet. And while I listened to them, offered sympathy and support and referrals, gave out addresses of shelters even more squalid and dangerous than the streets where they lived, I heard it.

Zzzmmmmmmmmm.

Joy.

Mom calls to ask if I can bring her something, but she can't remember what it's called.

"Come on, Angela, you know what I mean. It sounds

tense and desperate. A clench?"

"A clutch," I said.

Mom sighed. "That's the one. Bring me my clutch, the red one."

My mother's apartment is in Outremont, a few blocks away from the house where I grew up. On my way down Champagneur I spy three quarters of a smoke by the curb. It looks like a skeleton finger beckoning to me. I bend for it and as my hand goes out, a word floats down from above.

"Hello."

I look up to see a young Hasid, maybe sixteen, with clear quartz skin and reddish curls showing from under his fedora. Those hats look sharp and I don't care who knows it. "Hi," I say, closing my hand around the butt and slipping it into my pocket.

"Are you Jewish?" he says.

"No," I lie, thinking he will leave me alone.

"Do you speak Yiddish?"

"No."

"Do you speak French?"

"No."

"English?"

"No," I say, beginning to feel like I'm in an Abbott and Costello routine. I turn to go, but the kid halts me by going "Ah ah" in a sharp voice and raising his hand. I turn back.

"Listen," he says. "I need you to tell me about sex." His eyes are serious, pleading. He has that accent.

This is not the first time this has happened. I've been asked to explain blow jobs and finger-banging to teenage boys in black hats ever since my family moved to this neighbourhood. Once an older man asked me to come home with him, and seemed genuinely surprised when I declined.

"Why not?" he said. "I'd pay you!"

"I don't think I'm supposed to do that," I tell the kid, looking around. A man halfway down the block is smoking on his balcony. His eyes are shaded by the rim of his hat.

"I really have to know," he says. He seems so sad. What must it be like, to have wet dreams and no internet? I decide to be a grown-up about it.

"Okay." I take a deep breath. "There's a penis and a vagina—"

"Yeah yeah yeah," he says, waving his hand. "But is it fun?"

"Well, it helps if you like the person."

"You only have to *like* them?"

"Some people think you should love each other, but lots of people do it just for... fun."

He nods. Then he says, "is it big?"

"Is what big?"

"The hole."

"Uh. It's big enough, I guess. You know, it's not just, like, a hole."

His eyes widen. "What do you mean?"

"I mean it's like... got skin around it, and lips, and—"

"*Lips?*" I can see now this was the wrong thing to say.

"Can I see it?" he says.

"What?"

"The hole, can I see it?"

"No."

"Why not?"

"Because," I say, and start to walk away.

"Please," he says, and reaches for my arm. I start to run.

"You're so pretty!" he yells after me.

I run all the way to my mom's apartment, three blocks. I use the spare key to let myself in. The silkscreened

People's History posters on the wall have been re-arranged according to colour: Judi Bari, Cochabamba, the People's Occupation of Alcatraz, Emma Goldman, Little Bighorn. It's just like my friends' college dorm rooms, except my mom's posters are dry-mounted, not stuck on with Blu Tak. I notice a new sticker on the fridge: *No Love on Stolen Native Land*. I locate the clutch, which is really more of a purse, beside the bed, buried under the plain white comforter.

As I leave the building I do a quick scan for the kid, but he's either gone or in deep camouflage. Beyond the corner is the kosher bakery, which I can smell a block away. I decide to pay a visit for the first time in years.

A tiny woman behind the counter hustles rugelach and cheesecake and poppyseed rolls into crisp, thick brown paper bags. The crowd shouts out requests in what seems like total anarchy; there is no line, no numbers taken or called. Crumpled bills and handfuls of change flow back and forth over the glass. The smell is trance-inducing: yeast, sugar, eggs, the chemistry of rising and expansion.

I hover near the back of the scrum, waiting for an opening, trying for eye contact with the tiny woman. A short, pudgy, well-dressed man elbows past me and cries "I need some rugelach!"

I am startled by an older woman who touches my arm just above the elbow. Her pale hair peeks out from under a blue terrycloth turban. She is tall, though stooped, and wears a shapeless navy coat. The whites of her eyes are the colour of old snow.

"You had better just get in there," she says. "Since the war we don't stand in lines no more."

The heat from the rugelach spreads through my backpack into my lumbar region. On Côte-Sainte-Catherine the leaves are already beginning to turn. This fall everyone is wearing something called a shrug. It is like a special covering for the gesture; it only covers the part of the body that shrugs. The bus is late, or early. I paw the butt out of my pocket, put it in my mouth and light it.

The year I started smoking cigarettes I found on the curb was the year my dad started sleeping with The Turtle's wife. My sister Stacey and I boycotted our mom's feminist Seder and in retaliation Mom started having her DIY gynecology meetings in the living room. Once I found her looking at our neighbour Ms. Knope's cervix with a speculum, right on the green leatherette La-Z-Boy. There were a bunch of other women sitting around drinking herbal tea and gin—I could smell the juniper. Angela, come see this, Mom said, it looks just like a mini-doughnut. Dad was out somewhere, probably banging The Turtle's wife.

Sometime during that period I walked down Van Horne to the corner of Wiseman, right into a half-smoked cigarette, which I picked up and started huffing without even thinking about it. It was so natural, that first time; I've tried, unsuccessfully, to get back that feeling of spontaneity. No, not spontaneity—*need*. I went for it like one chemical bonding with another. I was twelve.

The Turtle wasn't called The Turtle because of some sex thing or because he refused to come out of his shell. He was The Turtle because he played one on television. Terrence was his name, Terrence the Turtle. He was the goofy, lumbering nemesis of the rabbit in a long-running series of commercials for O'Hare Couriers. His sidekick was a snail named Susan, and there was a running gag about how he couldn't keep up with her fast-paced lifestyle.

He had once been a serious actor, once played Lenny in a Stratford production of *The Homecoming*. But no one called him Lenny.

It was hard for me to imagine anyone marrying or even fucking him, and I guess it was hard for The Turtle's wife too, because from what I heard my dad wasn't the first or only person she slept with during the course of their marriage.

The cigarette habit, at least, proved to be a relatively long-term affair. I liked the surprise of it, the feeling of being a tourist. Would it be a lung-busting King Size Export 'A' Green, or "one-way-ticket" as Dad called them? A husky blue-collar Pall Mall? A prim and bitchy Menthol 100? More than once I was delighted to taste the medicinal green from a half-spent cig. I carried a lighter in my cargo pants everywhere I went.

There were also the times I would find a butt still burning, recently ejected from its owner's lip, sometimes still damp and salty at the end: the unexpected rush, the participation in the moment, the tongue-coating tang of a stranger's mouth.

"Hepatitis!" Stacey used to shout at me whenever I'd make a dive for a fast-rolling butt on its way to the gutter, flecks of orange scattering from its head. I learned to make my grabs alone.

We had grown up watching The Turtle's commercials, had stayed with him through bad writing, poor costume choices, short-lived sidekicks of unidentifiable species and gender. We would linger on the channel if we landed on one of The Turtle's ads. Already nostalgic for our childhoods, we felt a tenderness toward him and his message of slow-and-steady-wins-the-race. We would boo the rabbit, a grinning plushy forever knocking Terrence on his shell.

Stacey walked around in heels and Dad's tweed jacket, her mouth smeared with Cherry Pop! lipstick. At ten she looked like a tiny drag queen. She called The Turtle's wife Spare Mom. This was an attitude she had cultivated in recent years, much removed from the girl so sensitive she cried when someone said she was a southpaw.

Sometimes I wondered why Mom put up with this tacky business, Dad running out at eleven p.m., bizarre phone calls in the middle of the night.

"Look," said Mom. "You think you understand everything, but you don't. You think this sounds like nonsense. Yes, I can tell by the way you're frowning. You think you understand what love is, a prize you find at the bottom of the cereal box. You have no idea."

"You always told us love was a construct of the bourgeoisie," I said.

"We don't eat cereal," said Stacey, "because it overloads the pancreas."

"You're killing me," Mom said, "oh you're killing me. I'm dead."

The cooled air of the hospital smells like a pretty girl's hair. I pass the nurses' station, on which there is a coffee cup with a picture of a coffee cup on it. Two nurses are deep in conversation.

My mom is sitting up in bed, glaring at the TV. Her bald head and hooked nose give her the look of a wounded eagle. I'm relieved she isn't wearing her wig, a brown bobbed thing made for someone half her age. It has short Bettie Page bangs and is made from real hair, probably from some poor Russian woman forced to sell her ponytail to feed her kids. The wig was chosen by my mother's nurse, a tall, big-boned woman named Linda. Linda herself has a straight brown chop that hangs over her ears like two mud flaps. Her hands are very large and seem to have at least one more joint than normal. She has a deep voice that contrasts with her little girl mannerisms, like twirling the hair by her ear as she talks. Her eyes are green and striking.

Once she told me she had a new invention for dental floss.

"Oh yeah?" I said.

"Yep. Wanna know what it is?" Before I could answer, she said "Cinnamon buns!"

"As a flavour?" I said. My mother, who was sitting out of Linda's line of sight, caught my eye and made a loop-de-loop gesture by her temple—the international sign for total fucking nutbar.

"Nooooooo," Linda said, drawing her lips up into a smooch. "For cutting them! Because a knife gets too sticky."

"Wow," I said.

"Wow is right!"

There is something new and bizarre in the corner of the room, a face made out of what looks like bread dough, with blank holes for eyes and a tangle of curly yellow yarn on top like a kid's drawing of pubic hair. Paper wings protrude from either side of the head like scalloped ears. It's holding a wooden placard that reads *Friends are angels that come from above. Sent down from God for you to love. So if you are sad and don't know what to do. Just remember that I care for you!* I have no idea how it got there. It must have been left by the woman who occupied the room's other bed, who is no longer there. I try not to think about where she might be now.

The whole scene is making me feel terrible for my mother, who hates sentimentality like poison. "I know a woman," she once told me, "who saved a noodle that fell out of the pot and onto the red-hot burner and didn't burn. She framed it and hung it on the wall so its message could inspire her. I am doing everything I can not to become that woman."

Myself, I'm trying not to become the noodle.

"I brought rugelach," I say, holding out the bag.

"Oh God, take that away," she says. "I can't so much as look at food right now."

"Okay."

"Thank you though."

"I brought a book too. There's a new Chomsky I thought you might like."

"How sweet. Put it there." I start to put it on the night table, but she gestures toward the drawers. "No, no, in there," she says, "I need that clear, for my dinner tray."

"But how will you read it?"

"Well I'll get it out when I'm ready for it, dear, obviously." Which I have to admit is reasonable enough.

When Stacey and I were kids Mom used to give us a morning glass of apple cider vinegar cut with water. Drinking it was mechanical enough, though sometimes it would have a slimy gob of mother at the bottom. It was like swallowing an oyster. I would grimace as it slid sown my esophagus; it seemed like I could feel it the whole length of its journey to my gut.

"Why do they call it mother?" I asked once.

"Because it's the omnipotent wellspring of reproduction and health," said Mom.

"Because it's supposed to be good for you but makes you want to barf," said Stacey. Mom smiled and put her hands on our shoulders. "You'll thank me for this one day," she said, like a mom on TV.

Stacey and I started referring to her as Omnipotent Wellspring after that. We didn't call Dad anything.

Now my mom says "I'm dying for a fag."

"Mom, you can't say that."

"I believe I just did."

I fumble out a smoke from my pack. She puts it behind her ear, a gesture that recalls a younger version of herself with a pencil, hunched over her desk, making sketches for an illustration for *Tikkun* or *Mother Jones*.

"Remember how Leanne's working on the set of *The Man of Ville Emard* as a dresser?" I ask her. "The director told her she was so beautiful he's going to make a part for her in his next film. Isn't that hilarious? What a sleaze."

"Why would she tell you that?"

"Because it's funny?"

"It's a bit vain, no?"

"I think she just thought it was an amusing story."

"'You're so beautiful I'm going to put you in a movie.'"

"That's what she told me."

"To be funny."

"Yes."

"Is that really what you think?"

"Yes."

"Well. Maybe you're right. Some people need to pump themselves up to feel good, though."

"Mom!"

"I just think that maybe Leanne is a little insecure, and that's why she tells you these things. She's nowhere near as pretty as you are."

"This isn't about me! And, excuse me, she's ridiculously pretty. Everyone thinks so."

"If you say so."

"What?"

"If you say so."

"Okay. Forget I brought it up."

We sit in silence for a while.

"What in the name of God *is* that," I say, pointing to the angel.

"What?"

"That hideous angel."

"Oh," Mom says, "someone here gave me that. I thought it was kind of cute."

"It looks like a demented muffin."

"It's not hurting anyone, is it?"

"It's hurting my eyes." My mother says nothing, and I decide to drop it.

She had a particular way of telling Stacey and I we were getting in her hair. "No thanks," she'd say if we started a band with a blowdryer and a xylophone. Her tone was light, cordial, final.

"Well what about if we practise in the garage?"

"No thanks." Like we were Girl Guides with boxes of cookies. She never laughed at jokes but instead would say "That's funny." She could almost understand what makes people normal, but she couldn't be it.

"Stacey been by today?"

"Oh, not yet," she says, "She was here last night with that new lady of hers."

"Camille? The little kid from down the street?"

"Not so little anymore."

I nod. I remember Stacey and Camille holding hands, practising steps for an Israeli dance they learned at summer camp.

"I met someone," Mom says.

"You met someone? What does that mean, you met

someone? At a nightclub?"

"Don't be mean. Here, on the ward. His name is Bruce, and he's very nice. He's a teacher."

"So you, what, go on dates to the vending machine? Wash each other's bedsores? Do they provide special rooms for conjugal visits?"

"For godsakes Angela, we're friends. And he's married." But she's laughing.

"Never stopped you before."

"Angela Davis Feldman! Hush your mouth!"

"Did Brucie give you the angel?"

"Oh God no, not his style whatsoever." She can't stop giggling. Linda breezes in, bringing a chart and a sharp peppery smell.

"Well look at you gals, having a grand old time in here," she says, checking the numbers.

"Linda," says my mom, "My daughter was just admiring that sweet angel you gave me." Of course it would be Linda who gave it to her. She probably has a whole drawerful of them at home.

"Yes, it's lovely," I say. I try to catch Mom's eye but she just looks at me with a flat, over-pleasant smile.

"Well I just think a room isn't a room without an angel's touch."

"It's stunning," my mom says, a word I've never heard her use.

"Yes," I say, "I am definitely stunned."

"You know, there are angels all around us," Linda says.

I widen my eyes and nod, trying to look credulous. "Really?"

"Oh yes. This place is chockablock with them." Linda straightens up and looks at my mother with shock.

"Abigail! You're not wearing your hairdo!"

My mom's hand flies to her head. "Oh, I forgot to put it on!"

"Let me get it!" cries Linda. She and Mom bumble around like a couple of soft-shoe comedians, looking for the wig (my mom's bumbling being mostly with her hands), until Linda locates it in the bottom drawer of the dresser. "Now what were you doing there, you silly thing," she says. As Linda goes to fix it on my mother's head, she finds the cigarette behind her ear. "Abby! Naughty girl." She shakes the cigarette at her like a finger. My mom does an "Oops, I did it again!" face and they both laugh like teenagers.

Linda spends a good deal of time straightening the wig on my mother's head, her tongue protruding slightly from her mouth. I don't know where to look while she does this; it's like watching your relatives kiss.

"Ohhh..." she says. "There you go. Now you look absolutely stunning. Like a famous actress." My mom smiles and lowers her eyelids. She actually seems to be blushing. She's like a hothouse orchid, blooming under this woman's care.

"Really," Linda says, "you do look just like an old movie star. Who am I thinking of? Garbo? Katharine Hepburn? Who does she look like, Angela?"

"Yul Brynner?" I say.

They both look at me. My mom's eyes are blank as cups of coffee. Linda's have a bottomless shine—what is it? Pity, I think.

"Your daughter is so funny, Abigail," she says sadly.

"Yes," my mom says, "she's a riot." She gives me a tired smile.

"Whatever," I say.

"Clara Bow! That's it, that's who I was thinking of."

"Oh, I loved her in *Dangerous Curves*."

"Me too! They don't make them like that anymore, do they."

The hospital doors slide open. The Wellspring. The Omnipotent Wellspring of Reproduction and Health. I walk down the hill, my skin itching from sun and something else, something slow and heavy and inevitable. I feel for the sliver of joy.

A father and a little kid go by, the dad angrily marching ahead, the kid racing to keep up, babbling in that way kids do when they know something is terribly wrong but they don't know how to fix or even name it.

"But Dad, you know what?" the kid says. "Do ants have money?"

Halfway home I see the Hasid kid again, sitting on a swing in the kiddie park. He's trying to swing but you can tell he doesn't really get the mechanism. His legs go out at the wrong time and he doesn't lean into it. I try not to make eye contact, and when he calls out I keep going. "Wait," he says, "please." I turn around, careful. He's reaching into a pocket of his deep black coat. He pulls out a pack of cigarettes and waves them at me.

"You can have them," he says.

"For what?" I say.

"Nothing. They're for you."

I hesitate.

"Don't you like this kind?"

"Charcoal filters," I say.

"Is that good?"

"Probably not." I step forward and reach for them. He

shakes his head and gestures for me to hold out my hand. I do, and he drops the pack into my palm.

"Thank you," I say. He ducks his chin and starts to walk away.

"Hold on."

"Yeah?"

"You still want to see it?"

"Yeah?"

"Let's walk."

My mom's apartment is only a few blocks away. The kid looks around with interest. Probably he's never seen what his people look like in other habitats. "Where do you pray?" he asks. "Everywhere," I say.

I've done things I would prefer to hide from God. One night I rushed to the pharmacy to get the morning-after pill—it closed at eleven. It was a race against sperm. Outside I saw my old lover, Phil, locking up his bike. A fat messenger bag hung from his shoulder, which I knew meant he was delivering drugs to one of the bare-walled second-floor apartments on Mont Royal. We nodded to each other and asked no questions, as two people do when they are about to commit abominations.

The pharmacist asked when was my last period. "Two months," I said, "but that's because I voluntarily terminated a pregnancy." She looked at me like yeah, I know, I'm a reproductive disaster myself. Did I have any more questions?

"Can I drink with these pills?"

"Well, try not to throw up."

"Okay."

"If you throw up you'll have to take them again."

I gave her the thumbs up and got back on the street, a

precious plastic vial rattling around my bag.

But this wasn't one of those things.

"Do you want to have sex with me?" I say when it seems like a reasonable moment to do so.

"Aren't we already?"

"Well, yeah, I guess, but I mean like sex sex."

"Oh," he says. "Sex sex."

His cock is long and thin and narrows a bit before the head. He gets so hard that when we fuck I can hear it clicking against my cervix. It sounds unlikely, but it's true; it's one of those half-sound-half-feelings, like snapping your fingers. His skin is fine-grained and reddish. It hardly seems like skin at all. He smells only a bit like teenage boy. Mostly he has a vitamin B smell, like garden soil.

Later we share a smoke on the balcony. He is fully dressed again except for the hat, which is sitting on my mother's nighttable, like a game of One Of These Things Doesn't Belong Here. I decide it's confession time.

"My mother is dying," I tell him, "and my father lives with The Turtle's wife."

"The Turtle?"

"Never mind. So is this like a normal Hasidic thing to do? Are you kind of like the Amish in that way, where for one year you get to—"

"Shhhh," says the kid, putting his dirt-smelling hand over my mouth. "Do you hear that?"

"What," I say. And then I hear it.

Zzzmmmmmmmmmm.

A Favour

Lynnie has to quit her job as an abortion doula because she's pregnant. She's not showing yet, but it won't be long, and she's worried the sight could upset her clients.

"Don't get me wrong," she tells her roommate Alice, "most of them know exactly what they're doing. But they feel judged enough by the rest of the world. They don't need me resting my belly on their arm while they're in the stirrups."

She's worked at Full Spectrum for six years now and doesn't have a clue what other kind of jobs there are. She started as a volunteer and now sees up to ten clients a week. When she tells her boss that she's leaving for good she gets a slightly mechanical hug and a small cactus.

"Sorry to lose you, kid," says Miranda.

"I'll miss you guys," says Lynnie.

Miranda also gives Lynnie two letters of recommendation in unsealed envelopes, which Lynnie puts in her desk drawer. As she shuts it she wonders who is going to care about her commitment to women's wellbeing, her compassion, her strong work ethic and excellent punctuality record.

On her passport it says "masseuse" and that's pretty much the truth of it. She's considered just putting "doula," but the foreign-sounding word combined with her brown skin and curly black hair could equal hours of tedium in an interrogation room at the border. So she puts up with the winks and the jokes about happy endings and mostly gets an easy pass.

However, the passport thing gives her an idea.

She calls Raelle, who works at one of the rub-n-tugs on Ste-Catherine.

"Do you think you could get me a job at Renaldo's?"

"I don't know. Are you good with your hands? Can you do intensive body work?"

Lynnie thinks about the hundreds of shoulders she's rubbed, hands she's held, shiatsu pressure points she's activated over the years.

"Yeah," she says. "I think I can handle that."

Lynnie loves the unbridled silliness of the peeler joints on Ste-Catherine. In the small Ontario town where she grew up, the strip clubs attempted discretion, a demure classiness; they were called Gentleman Jack's and Snifters and The Treasure Trove. They had fake Doric columns and fake marble ashtrays and fake palm fronds hanging over the door. Here in Montreal the clubs have names like Sex Box, Sex Castle, and Supersex. Neon women in breast-baring bat costumes circle the signs, their dazzling LED nipples blinking like radio towers. On one sign a cartoon woman in a G-string mouths the words "*Le sex: j'aime ca.*" She reminds Lynnie of the naked ladies she and her brothers would draw as kids, with startled, spherical breasts. There is something touching about the naive crudeness of the image.

Although there is a power too in these superhero sex workers. Their lips are glossy and their heads thrown back, their breasts float as though suspended in heavy liquid. They are vibrant, these radioactive women, they light up the streets like rocket fire.

She meets Raelle outside one of the clubs, and they go into the Second Cup on the corner.

"I came up with a new package today," Raelle says. "It's called the VIP. What it is is I get them to take a really long shower, and then I towel them off."

"Yeah?" says Lynnie.

"It costs two hundred and twenty dollars," says Raelle. They both laugh, and Raelle starts singing along with the muzak on the café's sound system in an amazingly melodious and sultry voice, making up lyrics as she goes.

Baby don't you worry
Mama ain't gone away
She's coming back to towel you off
Just like when you were a babe
A babe in diapers, barely nursin
Cause you are a
Very
Important
Person

Raelle's boss is named Desmond. He stares at Lynnie for a long time before taking down her name ("Priscilla") and phone number.

"So Priscilla," he says, "what are you anyway? Greek or something?"

"Or something," says Lynnie.

"Anyway it's no biggie," Desmond says, "the patrons like variety. It's a regular bag of skittles around here." He winks at her, and she smiles in return.

Lynnie's phone makes a sound like bubbles popping. She unfolds it. It's Renaud.

"My hand moved in physio today."

"Renaud! That's wonderful!"

"Yeah."

"I'm so glad."

"Yeah. Soon I'll be playing again."

"Well that's just. Wonderful."

Many years ago Renaud was apparently a well-known musician. He was part of a boy band sensation, sort of the Quebecois answer to Menudo, called *Gare Garçon*. This translates as something like "boy station," which is maybe why the band had limited success within the province. Now in his late sixties, he is the super of her apartment building, occupying the first floor with his two dogs, inveterate crotch-sniffers named Chip and Mario. Every time Lynnie enters or leaves the building they charge her, noses aimed at her pants seam like heat-seeking missiles. "Get out of there," Renaud will shout. It seems like the classy thing to do would be not to call attention to it, but Renaud always makes a big deal. "Get out of there, fellas, leave well enough alone." Lynnie doesn't know how she feels about her crotch being referred to as *there*, as though it's a destination, something you could find on a map. As in, how do we get there? Are we there yet?

Renaud asks, "is that your bike locked up to the fence?"

"With the blue handlebars?"

"No."

"Then no."

"I was going to say you should move it under the balcony. It's bike thief season, you know."

"I do."

"And. Uh. Montpellier wants the rent by the fifteenth at the latest."

"Yeah. Yeah. I'm on it."

"Otherwise he says he'll contact the *Régie*."

"He won't have to."

"Goodbye, Lynnie."

"Goodbye, Renaud."

He's a handsome guy in that silver fox kind of way, with an oily half-black pompadour that's creeping further and further back on his skull. Deep lines around his mouth. A stroke froze his right arm this past winter and left his mouth a little crooked, which gives him a rakish air. When he tosses a ball to Mario or Chip they catch it in jaws that are agile and grasping as a pair of hands. He disliked Lynnie until he found out she was Iranian, not Haitian. "I got no beef with you guys," he said, "not like everyone else does."

What must it be like to get old? Her grandpa once described it like this: You're standing in line for the bus, but the line's long enough that it doesn't feel like standing in line. It just feels like walking around. But then, finally, from way down the street, you see the bus. And the line gets shorter and shorter, and you get closer and closer to the front. And then you know. You have to get on.

Guys, she had discovered, are weirdly attached to their sperm. When her former lover, Sebastian, turned her down she didn't speak to him for two months. "For fuck-sakes," she said in their last conversation, "you jerk off like five times a day. What's the difference if one time you stick it in a turkey baster?"

"I don't know," he said. "It would feel like my responsibility."

"It?"

"The baby."

"But it wouldn't be," Lynnie said.

"But it would *feel* like it."

She realized that she didn't want to be fighting someone over their bodily fluid; it felt like something out of Philip K. Dick.

"Fine. Whatever. Keep it. I don't want my baby to be a selfish jerk anyway."

So it's odd, then, for her to suddenly be faced with such an excess of semen. Her clients can't get rid of it fast enough, they have an unlimited supply in continual need of draining. It's an economics that Lynnie has never experienced before: supply and demand have become neatly concatenated in a single bodily function. She thinks of herself as a sales manager; her biggest concern is moving units. This is when she doesn't think of herself as a farmer, going to work in the wee hours of the morn to milk cows whose insistent lowing is painful to her because she senses their great need in her gut, where the tadpole hangs suspended in jelly.

Her belly is beginning to punch itself out from the inside. It's getting rounder and shiny-taut. If the clients notice they don't seem to care. Possibly she is the embodiment of some kind of fantastical uber-woman to them—mother and whore. She still puts on makeup and does her hair to go to work, even though Raelle tells her not to bother. "They like the just-rolled-out-of-bed thing," she says. "It makes it seem more intimate." Raelle's own dreadlocked hair is pulled into a messy ponytail and she's wearing a white cotton undershirt and cargo pants.

Lynnie thinks about a comment her best friend Alex made to her once. He said, "Whenever I pass a hooker on the street, I'm like 'sorry, thanks but no thanks.' But then I feel bad about it."

Lynnie pulled her coat together at the neck. "What, you think they take it personally? You think their feelings are hurt?"

"Well, I mean, it's them I'm rejecting, right? On a very personal level."

"Prostitutes are *working*, Alex," Lynnie says. "They're not poor deluded women who somehow have the idea that every man in the world wants to fuck them. They understand that not all guys are johns."

Alex says nothing, and Lynnie feels the hot flush of embarrassment that comes with winning an argument.

But now she wonders if she was right. She is beginning to feel that she can see through men's clothing, through their skin, into their desires. What they want is to consume her. She can no longer make eye contact with strangers, she's taken to wearing sunglasses or pulling her jacket's hood low over her face when out in public.

She whispers to the tadpole. "I won't let them get you," she says. But really she knows she is talking to herself.

Lynnie's roommate, Alice, who Lynnie suspects of not being totally okay with her line of work, says she can probably get Lynnie hired at her job. Six mornings a week Alice gets picked up in a van and driven an hour outside the city, to an organic farm. There she spends six hours in a zucchini patch with a paintbrush, hand-pollinating the flowers. Due to the bee shortage, she explains, small farms have suffered terrible fruit and vegetable drop, since most of them refuse or can't afford the patented self-pollinating seeds the mega-farms rely on. Their only option is to hire people like Alice to hand-pollinate their crops. "I work with recent immigrants mostly," she says, "guys from El Salvador and Sudan and Lebanon. It's less than minimum wage but I feel like I'm helping out. Anyway it's a pretty easy job," she tells Lynnie. "Not too physically demanding and you're outside all day."

"I'll think about it," says Lynnie.

Raelle's thumbs work their way down Lynnie's forearm, moving the buried muscle in circles. Her hands are incredibly strong; it feels like she has ball-peen hammers in place of fingers. Lately Lynnie has been cramping up very easily. Alice tells her to eat more bananas and Alex offers a family-sized tub of IcyHot. It must be the fetus draining her energy like this. Though it could be that her job is beginning to enter her bones. When she senses that look of masculine hunger she feels she could be swallowed in a single slurp, like a Jell-o shot.

"I'm walking home from work last night," Raelle says, rubbing, "and I pass by this apartment. It's about four-thirty or five, I guess. And the lights are always on in this place, and it's in the basement, so I can kind of see right down into it, you know, without really trying."

"Uh huh."

"And the guy who lives there, every time I look in, he's either jerking off, doing lines of coke, or playing a video game."

"Ha."

"Okay, but so last night, I happen to glance in as I go by, and guess what he's doing?"

Lynnie has no idea.

"He's eating a pie, from the middle."

"From the middle?"

"Yeah."

"With a fork?"

"A *spoon*."

"Somehow that's the most unwholesome part," Lynnie says.

"I know. Don't lift your shoulder like that."

"Like this?"

"Better."

Many months earlier, Alex waited for Lynnie in San Simeon, just off the Main. As he watched the window a group of men in jeans and short jackets entered the café and sat down. They were Italian or Greek maybe, but to Alex they formed nothing so much as a great conflagration or manifestation of Man: Man in baseball hat, Man in bomber jacket, Ray-Ban Man with sturdy and stylish heavy black shoes. Where did one buy such shoes? Alex had no idea. They seemed a different species altogether. They were thicker than him, their hair was short and coarse, and close-up they would smell of man-smells, like Brylcreem? No, that was his grandfather's generation. These days it would be Axe, or Polo Sport, or Hugo by Hugo Boss. These Men occupied another landscape, another dimension parallel to Alex's but completely separate. Their conversations were on subjects Alex could not fathom, nor could he guess at their ages. What would it be like to be them, or to be with them? Alex imagined their thick hammy chests pressing up against other bodies. What kind of sounds would they make?

His friend Sally had scorned the idea of sexual difference to him, once, after he pointed out a women's magazine with its monthly boast of "New Positions Guaranteed to

Make Your Man Drool!"

"What do you think they are this month," he asked. "The Flying Buttress? Crouching Tiger Hidden Dragon? The Dow Jones Industrial Average?"

Sally just scowled. "All these ideas about different positions, different styles, different gender orientations," she had said. "We only have so many orifices, and there are only so many ways to stuff them. And everyone does it more or less the same. The toolbox is not infinite."

"How come it's all about orifices?" Alex had said. "You are such a dyke. What about surfaces, protrusions, tumescences? Don't they deserve a little love?"

"Fucking is fucking," she said, "cock or no cock. Within limits," she added after a pause.

Still, Alex could not imagine that what these men did with their wives and girlfriends, their mistresses, even with each other, if that was possible, was anything like anything he had ever done or would do with anyone. They were like characters from television, these Men, but here they were; they and Alex shared a café, somehow. Worlds that were less accessible to him than Indonesia, Australia, Greenland existed and intersected his at every turn. It was one of the great mysteries of civilization.

Now he watched Lynnie glide up on her bike, lock it to a parking meter outside. She had called him out of the blue, saying she had a proposal for him.

"What?" he had said.

"I have to ask you in person."

"Sounds kinky."

"Like you wouldn't believe."

She waved at him through the window. The door opened with a blast of autumn smell. As she walked past the table of

Men they stared unabashedly, like children. And Alex knew, before she even opened her mouth, that he would say yes.

Raelle walks Lynnie to the metro station after work. An older man in a tweed coat is coming towards them, holding an umbrella even though it hasn't rained in weeks. He smiles solicitously. "You girls shouldn't be walking alone," he says. "This isn't a good neighbourhood."

"We're not alone," says Lynnie.

"Still," he says. "There's bad men around. I could be a rapist. How do you know?"

"Well then maybe *you* should stay off the streets," says Raelle.

"I was just trying to help."

"Thanks," says Lynnie, as Raelle glares after him.

Raelle thinks about the first time she met Lynnie, at the clinic. None of the doctors or nurses wore uniforms, which made Raelle feel like she was in a Pilates class. She couldn't remember any other situation in which she'd been surrounded by women of various ages and shapes and ethnicities, all in comfy breathable cotton and elastic waistbands. In fact there was something YWCAish about the whole thing, the casual banter, the nonchalance about nudity and bodily functions. It was how she imagined a low-budget spa getaway to be.

The clinic had offered a special service, a doula, to accompany her during the procedure. She had refused, picturing a woman in many scarves placing crystals on her abdomen and chanting in a made-up language. But due to some clerical mix-up, when she entered the small clean room, aside from the doctor and nurse there was this woman with a great bush of black hair held back from her face by a bandanna.

She wore brown trousers and a green shirt. She smiled, showing front teeth that were whiter than the ones on either side.

"My name is Lynnie," she said. "I'm here for you." The way she emphasized *you* made Raelle feel like the other people were not there for her. Which, in a way, they weren't.

In the recovery room after, Lynnie sat with Raelle, feeding her saltines and orange juice.

"I am never ever having sex again," said Raelle. "Unless it's for money."

"Oh c'mon, it wasn't that bad, was it?" said Lynnie.

Raelle was still dopey from the sedative. "Do you guys ever use the vacuum to, like, clean up the place? After hours?"

Lynnie stared at her, then laughed, a great cackle that shook the curtain drawn around Raelle's reclining chair.

On the other side of the curtain two women were talking about what they were going to do when Club Boîte du Sexe closed down. Raelle had seen them in the waiting room together earlier. It was hard to tell who was there for the procedure and who was the support; they were both wearing those weird paper slippers they give you that are like some kind of test of your origami skills. Raelle started wondering if they were both getting abortions. Maybe one of them got pregnant, and the other one decided she wasn't letting her friend go through it alone, so she went out and got knocked up that night.

"No," said Raelle, "it wasn't that bad. A bikini wax hurts more."

Lynnie gave Raelle her cell number. "Call me if you're worried about anything."

"Cindy works at Cleopatra's now," one of the women said. "She says it's all the rage."

The next day, Raelle dialled the number from her room-mate's landline.

"Alex?" said Lynnie's voice.

"No," said Raelle. "This is Raelle. From the clinic, from... yesterday." For some reason her throat stuck on the word "abortion," a word she had always held inside her like a hard-won diamond. She swallowed. "I had an abortion at three fifteen?"

"Of course," said Lynnie, "sorry. Is everything okay?"

"No," said Raelle. She felt like if only she could hear that laugh again, everything would be okay.

"Are you in pain?"

"No."

"Are you bleeding?"

"No," said Raelle. "But I could use a drink."

There was a pause, then Lynnie laughed.

"I get off at eight," she said.

They met at an all-night diner that served a dark reddish coffee that tasted like armpits. The waitress had a faded tattoo of a fleur-de-lis and called them both "Cocotte."

"Listen," Lynnie said. "It happened to me once, this kind of occupation." She spoke a bit formally, as though this were a story she had told many times before.

"The thing, the embryo, or zygote, whatever it is at that stage, lodged itself in my womb and set down to busying itself with basic and then more advanced mathematics: addition, multiplication, exponentials. I started thinking of it as Unknown Quantity N, and then just N. My boyfriend wanted to call it Kevin, a name he hated. But to me it was N. N the Unknown. N the Destroyer. Because let's be real here: that thing was sapping my resources as surely and as thoroughly as a strip mine. I could barely stay awake with all that compounded math in me; I was dropping off in the middle of my classes. It would grow and grow and eventually tear its way out of me and if I lived or died, it could give two shits. It didn't love me. I was just a feedbag it had strapped on, a big nutrient-rich ball it was draining like a tick. I didn't understand how my body could act so completely and incontrovertibly against my wishes. It was a betrayal of the deepest order.

"I called the clinic and made an appointment. Three weeks was the earliest they could give me. I didn't know if I would make it that long; I kept thinking it would just burst out of me like the alien from *Alien* and run screaming through the kitchen while I expired in a puddle of corn syrup and red dye."

She smiled at Raelle and took a sip of her coffee.

"Then the accident happened," she said. "I was biking home one night from a movie; I had just crossed Sherbrooke and was picking up some speed when a car pulled out in front of me without checking its side mirror. Later I was told I flew five feet through the air, landed hard enough on the car's hood to knock the front bumper off, and then bounced to a landing on the concrete with my arms and legs splayed like I was making the most perfect snow angel, face down. All I remember is a crunch and then the odd sensation of looking up and seeing the ground.

"I came to in the hospital with a broken collarbone, a sprained wrist, a gap where my favourite teeth used to be, and some pretty gnarly bruises, but other than that I was miraculously unhurt. It also felt like I was leaking in some vital and possibly fatal way, but I couldn't move enough to see what it was. I tuned in and out to the doctor's lecture about how my helmet saved my life. Talk about preaching to the converted. Then she moved in closer and spoke in a low voice. 'You were pregnant. Did you know?'

"It was a double shock, hearing it out loud from a stranger and the use of the past tense. An affirmation and negation in the same phrase.

"'N,' I said, waiting for the outcome of the equation.

"'You miscarried,' she said.

"I didn't say anything.

"'It was very early,' she went on. 'Too early to know if the pregnancy was even viable. I'm sorry,' she said, 'I know it's a shock. But there's no reason why you couldn't have another, when you're ready. How are you feeling?'

"'N,' I said again. It must have sounded enough like an agreement or an admission of alrightness, because she straightened her shoulders and said, 'Well, okay, the nurse will be in to see you shortly. Good luck.'

"I know I should have felt a sense of loss, of grieving. The nurse had such big gentle eyes, touched me so carefully, as though I were an orphaned animal unaccustomed to human care. But what I thought was, *my body chose me.* When it came down to it, it considered me, Lynnie, whatever that meant, enough of a going concern to divert the resources needed to keep me alive. It was, in a way, the biggest self-affirmation I've ever had."

She leaned back in the naugahyde booth.

"Yeah," said Raelle. "Fuck having kids."

Lynnie looked to one side. "Well, I wouldn't quite say that."

This guy wants it fast. This guy wants it slow. This guy wants lavender-scented oil and this guy wants none. And this guy cries wee wee wee...

Lynnie hums nursery rhymes to herself while she works. It's become a tic that she's barely aware of, the way her feet seem to chant *come on, come on, come on* as she walks to and from the metro on nights when she's too tired or achy to bike. Her favourites are the ones about clever animals that outsmart a common enemy by working together; she's less keen on the princesses and ladies-in-waiting. Too much emphasis on clothes. In Montreal summer it makes her itchy just to think about bustles and corsets and hose and all those layers of silk and cotton jacquard. She thinks about pigs in jaunty hats, clever ants and idle grasshoppers, swashbuckling cats and silly geese. She would like to make a stencil for the tadpole's crib, but she doesn't think she'll have time.

"Guh," says this guy. Then, "thanks."

"No worries," says Lynnie as she runs a towel under lukewarm water. "See you next week."

"Check it out, the cat can talk," says Alice.

"No it can't," says Lynnie.

"Yes it can. Listen. Max, what's your weapon of choice?"

Arrow.

"Max, what's your favourite chocolate bar?"

Aero.

"Max, put your ducks in..."

A row.

"Okay, okay, I get it. Hilarious."

As Lynnie goes out the back door she sees Mario, Renaud's mastiff, leaping against his window. His bark is faint, muffled by the retrofitted double-paned glass. He leaps and leaps, his claws scrabbling against the glass, leaving long whitish smears.

Lynnie and Raelle ride home after the John Waters movie, in preparation for which they stashed a couple cans (ginger ale for Lynnie, PBR for Raelle) in their purses and gave each other razor-thin eyeliner moustaches. A few blocks from their apartment, a man steps out into the street and flags them down, waving his hands over his head like he's on a deserted island and they're an airplane.

"A favour," he says when they slow down. "It's a holiday."

The man is Hasidic. He wears a white shirt and a prayer shawl and those short black pants and stockings that remind Lynnie of Tintin. Instead of a black hat he has only a small matte skullcap. His sidelocks are almost totally straight and limp from the heat. Lynnie and Raelle look at each other.

"Come, come," says the man.

They dismount and roll their bikes to the fence outside the apartment. The yard is overgrown and weedy, with plastic toys scattered around. The man waits in the doorway. As they lock up, Raelle grabs Lynnie's arm and whispers into her face. *Moustaches.* They lick fingers and apply them to each other's upper lips. Raelle has a tenderness that Lynnie had not been aware of before.

"Am I good?" says Raelle. She has a faint brown smear, like she's been drinking hot chocolate.

"Yeah, you're good."

Lynnie and Alice's old landlord was Hasidic, and it took him three years to figure out who was Lynnie and who was Alice because he never looked either of them in the face. But this man is garrulous and friendly. He ushers Lynnie and Raelle inside, where his wife is smiling and nodding under a massive tinkling chandelier. "Thank you, thank you," they say.

"Would you like a drink?" the woman asks. She goes down the hall and into the kitchen, while the man smiles and nods at them. She returns with two plastic cups and a carton of Tropicana. In the kitchen doorway a couple of small girls appear in matching striped dresses, holding hands. They stare in eerie twinnish silence.

"Thank you," says Lynnie, taking the juice. It's cold and viscous, like shower gel.

The four of them stand in the hall smiling at each other, while the girls watch the strangers with big eyes. Finally the woman claps her hands and beckons for Lynnie and Raelle to follow her. Lynnie expects to be led to the kitchen, where one or another of them will turn the oven off or the air conditioner on. Instead the woman mounts the staircase, leaning heavily on the banister. Lynnie and Raelle follow, the man bringing up the rear. At the top of the stairs they are motioned into a bedroom.

In the bed is an old man, old-old, ancient, with papery wasps'-nest skin and eyelids that hang like dough over his red-rimmed eyes. He's wearing an oxygen mask connected to a hissing metal tank. The thinnest possible thread, no wider than a spider's filament, seems to connect him to the world. A small television sits mute in the corner of the room.

The woman smiles. "My daddy," she says. "A good man. A rebbe."

They nod.

"A serious man."

They nod. Behind them the husband is fiddling with something in a drawer.

"Now, he don't go out so much. He gets lonely."

They nod.

"A man, he needs certain things. Even an old man."

They nod.

"So?" she says, raising her eyebrows at them, expectant.

The husband has taken a black oblong object from the drawer and placed it on top of the bed, between the twin hills of the old man's feet.

Lynnie feels suddenly dizzy. She puts a hand on top of her belly, wishing she could somehow reach through the layers of skin and meat and grasp the fetus, which she imagines as cold and hard, like a china figurine. Nowhere, nowhere is she safe. With her other hand she grasps Raelle's.

"Listen," she says. "I don't think we can give you what you want."

Raelle squeezes her hand, hard. Harder than reassurance. She looks down. The object is a remote control. The woman is still smiling. Raelle aims it at the television, and a talk show clicks on.

"The thing about a talking dog is not what it's saying but the fact that it's talking at all," says a woman in a periwinkle pantsuit.

"Thank you," whispers the old man.

As they're leaving, Raelle turns to the woman. "*Zie gezunt,*" she says. The woman responds "*Gey gezunterheyt.*" She smiles and flaps a hand as they pass through the threshold.

"You speak Yiddish?" Lynnie asks as they unlock their bikes.

"A few phrases. Nothing real conversational."

"How did that happen?"

"Dad worked at a retirement home for Jewish seniors. He picked it up, I guess. Until I was twenty I thought *keyn-eyn-hora* was an old Trinidad expression."

A Hasidic man and his daughter, about twelve, are taking a night stroll around the block. The man waves at the two of them in a shy and friendly way. They wave back.

"Okay," Raelle says, "I gotta know. Who knocked you up?"

Lynnie smiles. "A turkey baster," she says.

"Oh c'mon," says Raelle.

"Look," says Lynnie. "Do you have, like, a really old comfortable T-shirt? And you'll probably never wear it out of the house, but you'll never get rid of it, because it fits you really well, and feels pretty nice, and... gets you pregnant? Okay, that metaphor fell apart."

"Fine," says Raelle, not crossly, "I get it."

Lynnie crosses her fingers behind her back and hopes Alex doesn't mind being called a T-shirt.

When Lynnie gets home Mario is still at the window, barking and leaping. She looks closer. There are streaks of blood on the glass, red drying to russet. She runs inside, holding her belly as she takes the stairs two at a time.

She and Alice watch from the balcony as Renaud, stretchered, is loaded into an ambulance. The neighbour, an older woman with hair dyed the colour of a Florida sunset, comes out on the adjacent balcony. She turns to look at the two women, pregnant Lynnie and sweat-stained Alice, with their arms around each other, brown bottles and potted herbs littering their small balcony. The ambulance lights reflect in her huge glasses and she stares at Lynnie and Alice with blinking red panels. She mutters something under her breath, then goes inside, slamming the door behind her.

"They're ginger ale bottles," Lynnie calls as an afterthought.

The first-floor apartment is thick with blue smoke and relatives. Lynnie realizes she had imagined Renaud a lone wolf, estranged from his family, an old coot with a grudge against the world. But his former home is packed with sisters, brothers, cousins, friends, nieces and nephews. There is even a daughter, who Lynnie never knew existed, with a handsome, possibly Haitian husband and a toddler chewing on a rubber toy. The daughter takes the sodden shape from the boy's mouth and considers it, and Lynnie realizes it's one of Mario's. She takes a scoop of *pâté chinois* from a pie plate and approaches the daughter, makes a weak French joke that the daughter smiles at. Her son clutches his mother's leg. He has Renaud's same eyebrows, cocky. Though maybe this is only wishful thinking on Lynnie's part.

"It's nuts to butts in here," says the daughter, Christine.

"Renaud had a lot of people in his life," says Lynnie, hoping she sounds neither trite nor incredulous.

"When are you due?" Christine asks.

"End of the summer."

"Are you scared?"

"Shitless," says Lynnie.

Christine takes her hand. "You're a strong girl," she says. "Renaud loved you very much."

Lynnie doubts Renaud has ever said such a thing to his daughter, but she smiles and squeezes back.

Alice and Raelle are talking to two of the brothers, wisecracking pot-bellied guys with easy laughs. Their names are Vincent and 'Tit Gars, and they tease Raelle about her dreadlocks, calling her Sister Marley. Normally Raelle would blacken an eye for such a thing, but she laughs and pokes Vincent in the belly and calls him the Pillsbury Doughboy.

One of the sisters puts on a Gare Garçon record and starts singing along.

Alex comes in from the balcony, his eyes red, his hair skunky. "You wouldn't believe the stories these guys have," he says to Lynnie. "That Pierre, he flew a CF-18 during the Gulf war."

"So what, that makes him cool?" says Alice. "Do you know how many civilians died in that war?"

"Over a hundred thousand," says Alex. "I should know, I helped organize the weekly demos against it."

"I went to those demos!" says Raelle.

"I thought you looked familiar," Alex says. Alice shakes her head.

The next song is up-tempo, with a pseudo-samba beat. Christine's husband comes over and takes Lynnie's hand and leads her into the middle of the floor. From the corner of her eye Lynnie sees Raelle dancing with Vincent, and Alex talking excitedly with 'Tit Gars and Pierre, making buzzing, explosive sounds with his lips. The husband twirls her, spins her out and then snaps her back. The tadpole is a gyroscope in her, keeping her upright.

The voices of the five young boys, old and gone now, blend and rise. "Cha cha cha," says Renaud.

"*T'es une belle danseuse!*" the husband tells her.

"No I'm not," she says.

Cha cha cha.

Publication Notes

Earlier versions of some of the stories in this collection first appeared elsewhere.

"Moving Day" first appeared in the limited edition booklet *Moving Day & Other Stories* (Paper Pusher, 2011).

"The Yoga Teachers" was broadcast on CBC Radio One in January 2010, and was published at maisonneuve.ca and in the anthology *Minority Reports: New English Writing from Quebec* (Vehicule Press, 2011).

"Last Man Standing" first appeared in the Summer 2011 issue of *Maisonneuve*, and was reprinted in the limited edition booklet *Moving Day & Other Stories* (Paper Pusher, 2011). A French translation (*Le dernier homme*, trans. Melanie Vincelette) appeared in *Zinc* No. 25. A recording of the story, read by John Dunn Hill, appears at annaleventhal.com.

"Sweet Affliction" was published in *Geist #77*, and was reprinted in the limited edition booklet *Moving Day & Other Stories* (Paper Pusher, 2011).

"The Polar Bear at the Museum" was first published in *Geist #67* in 2007 and subsequently republished in *The Journey Prize Stories 20* (McClelland & Stewart) in 2008.

A 500-word excerpt of an early draft of "Glory Days" appeared anonymously on the CBC Writing Awards website as part of the CBC Writing Challenge in fall of 2011.

Thanks

I extend my gratitude to the Canada Council for the Arts and the Conseil des arts et des lettres du Quèbec for providing me with funding to write this book.

Parts of this book were written at the Banff Centre for the Arts in Banff, Alberta, and the Roberts Street Social Centre in Halifax, Nova Scotia, and I thank them for giving me a place to rest my laptop, along with community and solitude in fair measures.

Thanks to Greg Hollingshead, Lee Henderson, and Oana Avasilichioaei, who gave this manuscript valuable guidance at an early, tender stage.

Thanks to my agent, Natalie St. Pierre at the HSW Literary Agency, for her unflagging faith in this book. And to Nic Boshart, Robbie MacGregor, Megan Fildes, and the Invisible team—the coolest dudes in the game. And to my editor, Michelle MacAleese, for her patience and sharp eye.

Michelle Sterling, Sean Michaels, Jeff Miller, and Melissa Bull: you are my eyes and ears. Thanks doesn't seem like enough, but here it is anyway.

To my parents, Paula Mitchell and Arnold Leventhal, for their next-level support and encouragement. And to Sarah Pupo, Taliesin McEnaney, Catherine McInnis, Alphie Primeau, Robyn Maynard, Carly Glanzberg, John Hodgins, Chloe Vice, Andrew Hood, Suzie Smith, and Caitlin Hutchison.

INVISIBLE PUBLISHING is a not-for-profit publishing company that produces contemporary works of fiction, creative non-fiction, and poetry. We publish material that's engaging, literary, current, and uniquely Canadian. We're small in scale, but we take our work, and our mission, seriously. We produce culturally relevant titles that are well written, beautifully designed, and affordable.

Invisible Publishing has been in operation for just over half a decade. Since releasing our first fiction titles in the spring of 2007, our catalogue has come to include works of graphic fiction and non-fiction, pop culture biographies, experimental poetry and prose.

Invisible Publishing continues to produce high quality literary works, we're also home to the Bibliophonic series and the Snare imprint.

If you'd like to know more please get in touch.
info@invisiblepublishing.com

Invisible Publishing
Halifax & Toronto